Moonlight in
Winter Park

SAMANTHA CHASE

ISBN: 978-0-9981064-2-7

ISBN: 978-0-9981064-2-7

Editor: Jillian Rivera
Cover artist: Dana Lamothe/Designs by Dana
Print formatting: Kim Brooks

Moonlight in
Winter Park

Chapter *One*

"You can't be serious! That's totally not fair!"

"I know, I know. But there's nothing I can do about it. My hands are kind of tied."

Hope slouched down on her sofa and pouted. "There has to be something you can do. It's Christmas, Ted. We always spend Christmas together and this year…well…it's important."

"I don't know how to get out of it. I know this year is going to be…difficult. Believe me, I want to be there with you but this is something that I have to do."

Somehow she doubted that. Her brother was a workaholic with no spine. Whenever his boss said "*jump*," there was Ted asking how high. "So now I'm going to be all by myself?" she asked incredulously. "I'm barely hanging on by a thread here."

"I'm sure you can find some friends to hang out

with. Don't be so dramatic," he said.

"Dramatic? Seriously? Ted, we just buried our parents two months ago. Christmas was always a big deal to us. How can you just blow that off, especially this year?"

He sighed loudly into the phone. "Look, you know how important my job is to me. Merry and I want to get married next year so we're both working extra shifts and doing everything we can to save some money. She's working the ER both Christmas Eve and Christmas Day, so when Mr. James told me he needed someone to work the holiday, I agreed."

Even though Ted couldn't see her, Hope rolled her eyes. "He needed someone? For real? Don't you mean he *demanded* that you work? That's more his M.O."

"Okay, maybe he said that either I had to work or half of the department would have to. I didn't want to do that to everyone, Hope. They all have families and I…"

"You did not just say that!" she cried. "You have family! I'm your family! Or don't I count anymore?"

"I'm sorry; I didn't mean it that way," he said, quickly backpedaling. "I just meant that…well…most of them have kids and I would hate to be the reason someone missed out on spending Christmas with them. I didn't want to be selfish."

Hope greatly doubted that was the whole truth but there really wasn't anything she could do about it. "I'm just really disappointed, Ted," she said sadly. "You're the only family I have and now I'm not even going to get to spend Christmas with you. It's not fair."

"I really am sorry. I thought I was doing a good thing."

For who? She sighed. "Maybe you can come by after work? I know it will be late but I can work with having a late dinner. What do you say?"

"I wish I could. I'm not even going to be here in town. Mr. James wanted to go and work from his lodge up in the mountains so that's where I have to be."

"This guy has a lot of nerve," she snapped. "Like it's not enough that he's making you work through Christmas, but he's effectively cutting you off from your family and your fiancée. What kind of beast does that?"

"Beast?" Ted chuckled.

"I could have said Scrooge, but it was too obvious," she said with a light laugh of her own. "But I'm serious, Ted. Why do you still work for this man? What kind of benefit do you get out of working for him? Can't you look for another job?"

"Hope, Mr. James gave me my start when no one else wanted to hire me. I was fresh out of college and he gave me a chance."

"Ted, please. You're a very intelligent man. You started out in an entry-level position and all he did was move you up to the job you actually wanted and were more than qualified for. You've been there for over five years already; it's not like he did you a favor."

"Maybe not, but I'm still grateful to him. I'm

on the verge of heading up a large account. If I can work with him one-on-one and show him that I'm capable, maybe I'll finally get that big promotion! I'm not looking at this situation as punishment, Hope, I'm looking at it as a chance to finally get the man's full attention!"

It was on the tip of her tongue to say that if the man hadn't really seen all of his potential in the last five years, then he probably wasn't going to see it now, but she held her tongue. It was a losing battle. There was no way that she was going to convince her brother to stand up to his boss and spend Christmas with her. She was going to be alone and she was going to have to deal with it.

That didn't mean she couldn't play a little dirty.

"Well, I guess I can understand that," she said with a sigh. "I better go. I just finished baking my second batch of cookies and they should be cool by now. I guess I'll talk to you…"

"Wait, wait, wait," he interrupted. "What kind of cookies did you bake?"

"Hmm, let's see. The first batch was my white chocolate oatmeal raisin cookies. They came out beautifully," she said with pride. "And I'm putting together the chocolate peppermint patty cookies now. I hope I have enough filling. I've tasted way too much of it!"

"Damn. Those are my favorites, too."

She sighed dramatically. "I know. I'll put some in the freezer and you can have them after Christmas."

"But that's so far away! Why do I have to wait until after Christmas?"

"I just figured that with your busy work schedule, you wouldn't have time to come over and have any."

Ted paused for a long moment. "That's true," he said. "But that just sucks. Why can't you drop by the office? Maybe we can have a late dinner or something?"

Hope looked at the clock and saw that it was only a little after five. Granted, it was a Saturday, but she wasn't even going to question what he was doing at the office, especially after the conversation they'd been having. "I don't know. Vending machine food really isn't very appealing."

"Oh," he said dejectedly. "I guess I was kind of hoping that you'd make something and bring it over. I can't even remember the last time I had a home-cooked meal."

Oh, brother. "Does Merry fall for that whole *'woe is me'* bit?"

He chuckled. "Sometimes."

And apparently Hope did too. "Okay, I'll tell you what. Even though I wasn't planning on cooking tonight since I'm so busy baking, I'll have pity on you."

"You will?" he asked excitedly. "Any chance you have the makings for some of your famous stuffed meatloaf?"

She laughed. "I think I can swing that."

"And mashed potatoes?"

"Who on earth would eat meatloaf without mashed potatoes? That would be a crime!"

"And corn?"

"Of course."

"And some cookies for dessert?"

"Now you're just getting greedy," she said but was excited at the thought of them at least having a little of time together. "Fine. And cookies for dessert. I'll be at your office around seven-thirty. Will that be okay?"

"Absolutely!"

"Okay. Then I better go and get to the store so I can meet all your demands," she teased.

"Hope? You're a lifesaver," he said seriously. "I'm not kidding. You're the best sister a guy could have."

"Yeah, yeah, yeah," she said lightly even though his words brought tears to her eyes. "I'll let you tell me how awesome I am over dinner. Now go and get some work done so that you can take longer than a fifteen-minute break with me."

"Done. And you don't have to worry. I'm the only one in the office today so we'll be able to hang out for longer than that."

"You promise?"

"Absolutely," he said. "I'll see you at seven-thirty."

❧

As Hope Cooper gently placed her loaded insulated bag filled with dinner in the car, she sighed. She hated this, the way their lives were going. At least Ted had Merry. If everything went according to Ted's plan, he and Merry would be married by this time next year and planning a family of their own.

And where would that leave her?

Alone. Utterly and completely alone.

Certainly not a happy thought.

The drive to the office complex where Ted worked took only fifteen minutes. James Enterprises was like a small city within itself and Hope often wondered how most of the employees found their way around. Ted often assured her that it wasn't all that complicated, but on the few occasions that she had been there, Hope had gotten lost.

That was why she preferred her own job; she worked from home, was her own boss and there was absolutely *zero* chance of her getting lost.

While Ted loved the pace and the challenge of working for such a large company, Hope couldn't see its allure. James Enterprises owned hotels and resorts all over the world. Some were luxurious, five-star hotels, while others leaned toward the quaint bed and breakfast type. Ted was a numbers guy, and he worked with a team of about two dozen others who helped to manage the financing for new resorts and projects on the existing ones. Personally, numbers made Hope's head hurt–*stupid math!*–but she was sincerely impressed with her brother's knack for them.

One of the biggest problems she had with Ted's job was the number of hours he had to work. Long days, overtime, weekends, holidays…it seemed endless. And was he compensated for all of those extra hours? Not as much as he should be. If Ted received the amount of money that he rightfully should for all of that time, well, let's just say that he and Merry would most likely be married by now and neither of them would have to cave in and work the holiday shifts that no one else wanted.

Personally, Hope blamed the elusive Mr. James. She snorted at the thought of him. G.B. James. What the heck kind of name was that anyway? For all the years Ted worked for the man, he still had no idea what the G or the B stood for. She didn't think anyone still made their employees use such formality in the workplace anymore but apparently this guy did.

Besides taking obvious advantage of her overworked brother, Hope's dislike of the man also hit on a more personal level. A year ago she had submitted a proposal to him regarding opening a small shop in one of his local hotels. It wasn't for anything big, but she had made a formal business proposal regarding opening a small café-slash-bakery. It had always been a dream of hers and when Ted had mentioned how the company was looking to open such a thing locally, Hope had immediately jumped on board. Unfortunately, Mr. Snooty G.B. James had rejected her proposal on the grounds that she was related to a member of the James Enterprises company and therefore it would show favoritism.

Seriously?

The rage had hit first, and then the disappointment. Ted apologized profusely for weeks after she had been rejected but it did little to make her feel any better. All it did was cement her belief that she just wasn't meant to have her little shop. Sure she could have looked elsewhere–other hotels, other locations–but she knew having the James Enterprises name behind her would have greatly helped her new business.

So she continued her work from home. Graphic design, web design, logos…it was fun and creative and it let her work in her yoga pants. Not a bad way to live. Still, it might have been nice to let her love of baking and cooking and, you know, being around other people come out and play. As of now she officially considered herself a hermit.

In comfy yoga pants.

Well, not now. Hope actually decided to put a bit of an effort into her appearance tonight. Just because it was Ted didn't mean he needed to see her looking all schleppy. While dinner was cooking, she'd taken the time to shower and do her hair–even using styling products–and dressed in a pair of jeans and a festive red sweater. Christmas was two weeks away but she loved it so and tended to embrace all things festive during the month of December. Okay, maybe starting back in November.

Early October, tops.

Pulling into the massive parking garage, Hope was thankful it was a Saturday. No parking attendant, no need to explain herself and wait for clearance. She parked the car and texted Ted that she was here. He wrote back saying he would let the security guard in the building know and he'd let her in and show her to the small kitchen area his department used.

At least they weren't going to have to sit in the massive cafeteria the building housed. She would have felt completely ridiculous with just the two of them sitting in a room that normally sat five hundred.

This was the first time she was going to get to go beyond the first floor and as much as she hated to admit it, the thought was a little exciting. She'd get a better glimpse into her brother's world and maybe see what all the fuss was about.

At the front entrance, a uniformed man in his early sixties smiled and opened the door for her. "Good evening, Miss Cooper. Your brother said you'd be stopping by."

A quick glance at his name tag gave Hope at least a name to go with. "Thank you and good evening to you, Jerome," she said with a smile. She waited while he locked the front door and then followed him over to the bank of elevators.

"Your brother asked me to bring you up to the eleventh floor. There's a nice kitchen area up there so the two of you can enjoy your dinner." He took a tentative sniff of the air and smiled. "I told him he should be thankful he has a sister who's willing not only to cook for him but to hand deliver it to him too."

Hope blushed. "You're more than welcome to join us. I made enough for a small army. I was figuring Ted wouldn't mind the leftovers but I'm sure he wouldn't mind sharing."

"Well that's very kind of you," Jerome said with a bashful grin, "but I have a lot of area to check on during my shift and I don't get a break until much later." He shook his head. "And it's going to feel like a long night because whatever you have in that bag smells heavenly."

She waved a hand at him as if to say "*oh, go on,*" but instead she said, "Well, feel free to stop up there later while you're on your break. If Ted's still here, you help yourself to whatever's left."

The elevator arrived on the eleventh floor and Jerome held the door while Hope stepped out. "Go down the hall all the way to the end and then make a left. The kitchen is the last door on your right."

"Thanks, Jerome. And have a good evening," Hope said with a smile.

"You too, Miss," he said and stepped back onto the elevator.

"What a nice man," she said quietly and made her way down to the kitchen. Once there, she texted Ted again to let him know where she was and he promised to be there in a few minutes. While she was waiting, she took the food out of the bag and began to set it up on the table. She even brought plates, silverware and drinks with her just to play it safe.

Testing the gravy, it felt a little cool to her so Hope walked over to the microwave, put it in, and waited for it to heat back up.

"What do you think you're doing?"

Hope spun around and saw a man standing in the doorway. Ted had said he was working all by himself so she had no idea who this person was. "I...I'm Hope Cooper. My brother Ted works here. I was just bringing him some dinner. He...he said it was okay."

The man looked at her oddly but didn't move from the doorway. "Ted told you it was all right to just come up here and make yourself at home?

11

How did you get in here?"

His words were a little curt and not at all friendly but Hope didn't feel the least bit intimidated. "Jerome let me in and escorted me up here. Ted said he'd be out in a minute." The microwave dinged that her gravy was ready. She smiled warmly as she held out her hand. "I'm Hope. And you are…?"

"Beckett," he said simply and accepted her handshake.

His eyes were a dark blue, almost black, and matched his hair. There was a dark shadow on his jaw that told Hope he hadn't shaved in a couple of days, at least. He was tall and his hands were large and for a moment she felt very small next to him. True, she was pretty short, barely five-four, but Beckett had to be at least six feet tall. He wore faded blue jeans and a black sweater and looked a little dangerous to her.

Carefully, she pulled her hand from his and took a step back. "Um…do you work with Ted?"

Beckett shook his head. "No. I don't believe I do."

"Oh," she said quietly and looked over her shoulder at the table she'd set. "You're more than welcome to join us for dinner. I invited Jerome too but he's not on break. If you'd like…"

He shook his head again. "Do you always invite people you don't know to dinner?" he asked, a trace of a smirk on his face.

Hope decided in that instant that this man should definitely smile more. When he was all serious and stern-looking, he was intimidating, but

when he smiled? He was really quite handsome.
"Not usually, but then again, I don't get out much."

That was brilliant, Hope, she chided herself.
Open mouth. Insert foot.

"What I mean is, I work from home and don't
make a habit of bringing dinner out to the masses."

He chuckled. "That's too bad because
whatever it is you've made for dinner smells
fabulous."

She blushed. "Thank you. It's one of Ted's
favorites and being how he's stuck working late
again, I felt it was the least I could do." She paused
and looked at Beckett and took in his casual attire.
"Is that why you're here? Are you being forced to
work overtime too?"

"Forced?" he asked as one dark brow arched.

Hope nodded. "Ted works crazy hours and
now he's being forced to work over Christmas. I
hate it. I wish this…Mr. James would
just…unclench and learn to treat his employees like
people and not like things he can control."

"I'm sure your brother could have said no,"
Beckett said mildly.

"No. No, he really couldn't. Apparently it was
either Ted work all through Christmas or the whole
department would." She sighed. "Now, thanks to
this deal with the devil, our Christmas is ruined."
She sat down at the table and frowned.

Beckett came and sat down beside her. "Surely
that's a bit of an over-exaggeration. I mean, I'm
sure you have other people to spend the holiday
with. Ted can't be the only person you were going
to see."

Hope looked at him and was mortified as tears began to well in her eyes. "He was. Our…our parents passed away a couple of months ago–car accident–and so it's just the two of us now. Well, Ted's engaged but his fiancée is working the Christmas shift in the ER for extra money." Turning her head away, she wiped away the tears that finally fell before turning back to him. "Sorry. I didn't mean to get all weepy on you."

Reaching for a napkin, Beckett handed it to her. "No need to apologize," he said softly. "It sounds to me like you have plenty of reasons to be upset."

Wiping away the last of her tears, Hope straightened in her seat. "I can't believe I just did that," she mumbled. "So, you never said if you're in the same boat as Ted–stuck here against your will."

"Sorry, but no," he said with a crooked grin. "I'm a bit of a workaholic and tend to put in the time without being asked."

"I can relate. Like I said, I work from home so I probably put in more time than I would if I worked for somebody else." She shrugged. "But it's my choice. Ted doesn't seem to have one."

Beckett looked at his watch and stood. "Maybe he should talk to his boss."

Hope came to her feet. "I keep telling him to but he won't. He feels very thankful for his job and doesn't want to rock the boat. I'm proud of him and what he does, but I just don't feel like all of his hard work is really appreciated."

"Not all bosses feel the need to pat their employees on the head," Beckett said a bit defensively.

Hope looked at him oddly. "I'm not saying to pat him on the head, but forcing someone to stay away from their family on Christmas and not receive proper compensation for it is a bit much, don't you think?"

Beckett looked at his watch again. "I really need to go. I hope you and your brother have a nice dinner," he said and smiled. "It was a pleasure meeting you, Hope." He took her hand in his and shook it. "Maybe next time you bring dinner, I'll be free to join you."

She couldn't help but smile. "That would be nice."

"Good night," he said as he released her hand and walked out of the kitchen.

Hope stood there, slightly dazzled by what just transpired. It had been a long time since a man had paid her any kind of attention and never had it been someone as handsome as Beckett. She tended to attract the computer geek crowd; there was nothing necessarily wrong with those guys but Hope didn't find them to be particularly exciting.

Unless you wanted to talk computer software until your ears bled.

Like she should talk. It wasn't as if she was a super-model herself. She was short, a little too curvy and her hair was always a bit out of control. Definitely not super-model material.

No, someone like Beckett was a definite first for her. He seemed to genuinely enjoy talking with her and seemed sincere when he mentioned having dinner with them if she came by again. She'd have to remember to ask Ted if he knew what department Beckett worked in and maybe she could coordinate another dinner before Christmas.

Beckett actually had a little pep in his step as he walked back to his office. It had been a long time since anyone surprised him in any capacity and Hope Cooper had just managed to do that. He'd had no idea anyone was in the kitchen and to find a beautiful woman standing there with food that made his mouth water was quite the pleasant surprise.

He knew he worked too hard and didn't go out and socialize much, but it was a conscious decision and one he couldn't regret. Did he miss dating? Yes. Did he miss just having some female companionship–hell, any companionship at this point? Yes. But as much as he would have loved to stay and spend more time with her, he wasn't the type of man to simply intrude on someone else's plans.

Especially family ones.

A shiver of distaste ran up his spine. It had been a long time since Beckett had spent any time with his own family and for good reasons. Granted, he knew not all families were like his, but he couldn't imagine what it was like to have a normal one. Maybe Hope had that kind of simple relationship with her brother, who knew? Beckett knew first-hand the kind of disappointment that came from being betrayed by the people who were supposed to love and support you.

Lesson learned.

Sitting down at his desk, he pictured Hope's smile. It was a beautiful one and lit up her entire face. He definitely wouldn't mind seeing her again but he knew things could get sticky because her brother worked for the company too. Maybe he'd see her around again. Maybe she'd come and have dinner with her brother another time. It made him wonder if she'd been here before and just hadn't noticed.

Now that would be a shame, he thought to himself, if a beautiful woman came around and he didn't even take the time to notice. He swiped a weary hand across his face. Something had to give, and soon. This was no way for a man to live. Long hours spent in an office with no social life to speak of was not how Beckett envisioned his life. Hell, he couldn't even remember the last time he went on a date, even a casual one.

Hope's face instantly sprang to mind. Maybe she was the proverbial sign he was looking for, someone to remind him how there was more to life than just work, just crunching numbers, just…existing. A sense of excitement that had nothing to do with closing a business deal swept over him. It had been a long time since he'd felt the pull of attraction and now that he had a taste of it, he wanted more.

Maybe it was time to step away from his desk a little more often and see what life had to offer.

"You are a lifesaver!" Ted said as he walked into the room. "I know I said it before but as I made my way down the hall, the scent of this meal was incredible." He kissed her on the cheek. "Did you have any trouble finding your way this time?"

She chuckled. "Jerome escorted me up here and then pointed me in the right direction from the elevator. He was very sweet."

"Poor guy," Ted said as he sat down and began doling out the food. "He should be retired by now but he can't afford to. His wife has health issues and they need Jerome's insurance to help with the medical bills."

"That's terrible! Shouldn't his retirement come with some sort of medical plan?"

Ted shook his head. "Apparently they don't offer that here."

Just another reason to hate G.B. James, she thought. Pushing the thought aside, she took her seat beside Ted and smiled when he put her plate of food in front of her. "I'm so glad you suggested this," she said. "We don't get so see each other nearly enough."

"I know, I know. Plus, this was a good way to get you out of the house."

"What's that supposed to mean?"

Ted looked at her with a frown. "Seriously? You're asking me that? You talk about how much I work but at least I work with other people. I get out of the house and socialize—even if it's just with my co-workers or the guy in the cafeteria, but at least I'm out there! You stay locked up in your townhouse and sit in front of a computer all day.

All of your correspondence with people is through text and email. Seriously, Hope, you have *got* to get out of the house more!"

"Eat your dinner," she grumbled and looked down at her own plate. "I don't have a reason to get out of the house more. My job keeps me tied to my computer. I can't help that."

"Then you need to cut back on your hours! Go out with friends or take a vacation or…something! Seriously, Hope, Merry and I are very concerned about you."

"You've talked to Merry about this?" she cried. "Why? Why would you do that?"

"Because you're my sister and I love you and I hate to see you hiding away in your house. You're a young woman and you should be out dating and meeting people, not sitting alone in your house."

"You know, just like your job is important to you, my job is important to me. In order to get my business to grow, I have to put in these hours. And, in case you've forgotten, I tried to change careers last year but your boss effectively cut my dream short."

Ted rolled his eyes. "Not this again," he said. "You could have approached other hotels, Hope. You could have looked for a storefront in other locations. James Enterprises wasn't the only option. You gave up too soon."

"Your boss criticized my business plan and then told me he wouldn't allow me the spot due to you working for the company. Or have you forgotten that first part?"

"I haven't forgotten and I don't particularly

think it was criticism. I think he merely pointed out how you needed a little more start-up capital in order to protect yourself. It was a helpful suggestion, Hope."

She made a face. "That's your opinion. I still think the man is a complete jerk."

"You have got to get over your hatred of my boss. This is where I work and I like it here. I'm not saying you have to like it, but I can't keep listening to you rip apart the man who signs my checks and whom I happen to admire. You need to just…move on."

"I might have if he hadn't gone and ruined Christmas."

"I'm not talking about this again," Ted said. After another bite of meatloaf, he put his fork down and took one of Hope's hands in his. "Dinner is fabulous. Thank you."

She knew he was changing the subject and she let him. "You're welcome. I have to admit, it's one of my favorites too and I don't usually make it unless it's for you."

"You brought dessert with you too, didn't you?"

She laughed. "I told you I would." Pulling her hand from his, she went back to eating her dinner. "So tell me about this big project that will have you working through Christmas."

"Hope…" Ted warned.

"No, I'm being serious. No condemnation. I was just curious about what you were working on. You sounded kind of excited about it when we talked earlier." She noticed her brother's hesitation.

"What? What's the matter?"

He sighed wearily. "Okay, but you have to promise not to get mad."

She frowned. "Why would I get mad?"

"We're re-addressing the café projects in some of the hotels."

"You have *got* to be kidding me!" she snapped, throwing her fork down. "So not only do I not get to see you for Christmas, but you'll be spending the time considering other people for the position I wanted? For real?"

"Look, I know it's not fair and if there was something I could do, I would. I'm not going to risk my job arguing about a policy that Mr. James has in place for a reason."

"Oh? And what reason could that be?" she asked sarcastically.

"I don't know," Ted said dejectedly. "I…I'm just sure there's a reason behind it. It seemed too random to just be in there for no reason. A lot of companies have a thing about nepotism. You can't fault him for that."

"Yes I can," she said firmly. "He employs thousands of people. I'm sure somewhere along the line there's a couple of people working for him who are related. You work here in the home office; I would be at one of the hotels. Our positions would be so far removed that there wouldn't be any issues. He's just a hardass who enjoys making people miserable."

"I knew I shouldn't have said anything to you about it."

"Well now it's too late. You already did.

Dammit." Her appetite gone, she pushed her plate away. "It's just not fair."

Ted stayed quiet as he finished his meal. When he was done, he sat back and studied his sister. "I'm telling you, you have other options. Have you talked to any of the other area hotels or to a realtor?"

"No."

"I think you're using Mr. James as an excuse not to take the risk."

"What?" she asked incredulously.

"You heard me. Changing careers is a big deal and there's a huge risk involved. I think that as much as you want to do this, you're scared. And I understand, I really do. But don't use this one rejection as a reason to not do it. Come on, Hope. What have you got to lose?"

"Um…my life savings?"

He laughed. "Please. You make a decent living and I've taught you to invest well. Even if the business didn't work out, you still have your graphic design skills to fall back on. You know mom and dad would have loved to see you open that café. Mom was thrilled when you asked if you could use some of her recipes."

The familiar sadness at the mention of their parents squeezed her heart. "I know," she replied quietly. "I don't want to let them down."

"Then you need to actually try. You know they believed in you. That's why they were willing to invest in the business. Come on. Promise me you will at least try. Make some calls. If there's nothing available that works for your budget then

I'll back off, but you have to do the research and ask some questions. Please, Hope."

Deep down Hope knew he had a point. "Okay. I'll make some inquiries this week."

Ted gave her a huge smile. "That's my girl!"

She couldn't help but smile back. "What's your schedule like this week? Any chance we can get together for dinner again but with Merry this time?"

"I've got a pretty hectic week," Ted said. "But maybe we could do this again next Saturday night here? I'll have to check and see what Merry's schedule is like but maybe if she's already scheduled, she can swap with someone."

"Here? At the office again? How do you know you'll have to work?"

"Trust me. I know," he said dismissively and stood to begin cleaning up their dinner dishes. "Any chance these leftovers are mine to take home?"

She shook her head and laughed. "Of course they are. Although, I did tell Jerome to come up and help himself on his break if you're still here."

"No worries. I wouldn't mind sharing with him." They worked together to get everything washed and packed back up and Hope pulled out the tins with the Christmas cookies in them.

"You've got a dozen of the peppermint patty ones and a dozen of the white chocolate oatmeal raisin. That should hold you over."

"Just until next week, right? You'll have more baked by then won't you? Different varieties?"

"I'll see how the week goes," she said and

placed the tins on the table next to the leftovers from dinner. "I have another tin in here that I was going to leave for your co-workers but I think I'll give them to Jerome if you don't mind."

"Not at all," Ted said as he opened one up and pulled out a cookie. "If only I had some milk."

"I can't believe you have any room left to eat anything," she said with another laugh. "You ate enough meatloaf for two people."

"Yeah, but in my defense, I haven't eaten all day."

She shook her head. "Don't tell me things like that and expect me not to have hater-rage toward your boss."

"You're going to have to get over it. Seriously." He took a bite out of the cookie. "No one else here feels that way and they actually work for him."

That reminded her... "Do you know a guy named Beckett?"

Ted finished chewing and shook his head. "No. Why?"

"It's nothing. He stopped in here before and we talked and I asked if he was being forced to work like you were and he kind of thought I was crazy too."

"That's because, whether you want to believe it or not, we all kind of respect Mr. James. He's a tough boss and he expects a lot but he's fair and we all enjoy our jobs."

Somehow Hope doubted that but she chose not to argue it anymore. It was an argument she was never going to win, so why ruin the few precious minutes she got to spend with her brother by fighting about it? "Anyway, he was working late today just like you but he said he didn't know who you were." She shrugged. "He seemed like a nice enough guy."

"Can I keep the insulated bag or do you need it back?" Ted asked rather than discuss the random guy whom he didn't know.

"I need it back for next weekend obviously. Just put all of your leftovers in the fridge and don't forget to take them home with you."

"Or maybe I'll just leave them here and then I won't have to go out to lunch this week."

"Aren't you afraid your co-workers will take your food?"

Ted shook his head. "Nah. It's not like that here. I've never had that happen."

"Well, don't forget I offered some to Jerome so if you're missing any, that's where they went."

"You're too good to everyone," Ted said and came over and hugged her. "I really need to get back to work. Thank you for bringing dinner over. I really appreciate it."

"It was my pleasure," she said and hugged him back. Stepping away, she gathered up the rest of her things and walked with Ted out of the kitchen.

"I'll call down to Jerome and let him know you're leaving. He'll keep an eye on you and make sure you get to your car okay."

"Thanks. I appreciate it. It's kind of a far walk from the door to the garage." It really was and although Hope wasn't normally the type of woman who feared walking around by herself, she also knew you couldn't be too careful. At the elevator, she kissed her brother on the cheek and said goodbye.

Down in the lobby, Jerome was nowhere in sight. "Hmm…now what?" She had no idea if she would trigger any kind of alarm by unlocking the door by herself. Looking around, Hope thought she heard footsteps coming and turned in that direction. She smiled, expecting to see Jerome. Quickly, she reached into her bag and pulled out the extra tin of cookies to give him. Her smile faltered for a moment and then brightened when she saw Beckett heading her way. She gave a small wave. "Hi."

"Hey," he said easily as he walked toward her. "How was dinner?"

"It was good, thank you. I was looking for Jerome. I wasn't sure how to get out of here without setting off any kind of alarm. Do you know where he is?"

"Actually, I think I saw him up on the third floor. But no worries, I can let you out of here."

"Oh. Okay," she said hesitantly.

"What? What's the matter?"

"Well, I was kind of hoping he'd walk me to my car. I know it sounds silly but…"

Beckett held up a hand and cut her off. "Say no more. Of course you shouldn't be walking around in the dark by yourself."

"It's well-lit out there," she said, "but still…"

Stepping around her, Beckett walked to the door, unlocked it and held it open for her. "After you."

"Thanks." Together they walked toward the

26

parking garage in silence. Once they reached her car, Hope stopped. "So…this is me."

Beckett smiled down at her. "I'm glad we made it here safely," he teased.

"Yeah, well…" She looked down and realized she was still holding the cookie tin. Her plan had been to give it to Jerome, but… "Well, thank you for walking with me. Here." She held out the tin to him. "Cookies," she said and then groaned at her own awkwardness. "I mean, I baked a ton of Christmas cookies. I brought a bunch of them for Ted and I made extras. So…here. For you."

Beckett looked at her and then the tin, but he didn't take it from her.

She blushed with embarrassment. "It's not a big deal. I mean, I was going to leave them for the people in Ted's department but I knew he'd eat them all before anyone had a chance to and then I thought I'd give them to Jerome." She shook her head and chuckled because she realized she was rambling. "They're not poisonous, I promise. I'm a really good baker. I swear. I just…well, you walked me to my car and I just wanted to say thanks." She continued to hold the tin in her hands and silently prayed he'd take it so she could die of embarrassment in the privacy of her car.

Finally–*finally!*–Beckett reached out and took the tin. His voice gruff, he said, "Thank you." He took a step back so Hope could open her car door and he waited until she was inside it and pulling away before moving.

In her rearview mirror, Hope saw him standing there and smiled. She gave another small wave and smiled even wider when he waved back.

As far as her Saturday nights usually went, she considered this one to be pretty darn successful and if she was really going to be optimistic, she considered her interaction with Beckett the closest thing she'd had to a date in a really long time.

Chapter *Two*

By the middle of the week Hope was feeling restless. True to her word, she had begun to make some phone calls to realtors to inquire about commercial real estate and storefronts in the area. All of the rents were way out of her league and it left her feeling more than a little discouraged. On top of that, she had baked dozens of cookies and realized she had no one to share them with.

Every year, Hope and her mom baked together in preparation for Christmas. Her parents always hosted a big Christmas Eve dessert open house and so it was the norm to spend every spare minute baking in the weeks leading up to Christmas. Now as she looked around the first floor of her condo, Hope realized she probably should have cut back a bit. There was no way she could possibly eat all of these and even if she split the stash with Ted, she still couldn't eat what was left.

Hmm...

Picking up her phone, she texted her brother and asked if she could bring some of the cookies by for his co-workers. He readily agreed but asked her to wait until after seven to come by the office. She shrugged it off and just figured he was busy. Looking around, she made a mental list of what to bring and remembered to bring an extra tin for Jerome since she'd given his to Beckett on Saturday night.

Beckett.

Hope actually sighed at the thought of him. She really needed to get out more if just one brief and completely boring encounter with the man had her still thinking about him four days later. Maybe she'd bring an extra tin of cookies.

Just in case.

With a renewed sense of purpose, Hope sprang into action. Quick shower? Check. Festive green sweater? Check. The jeans that made her butt look super cute? Check. Running around her bedroom thirty minutes later, she looked in the mirror and frowned. Hair. It was always the hair. Wild and curly and more than a little out of control, she considered her options. There was always a hat, but that raised the possibility of having to take off the hat while at Ted's office and everyone seeing what a mess she was.

No hat.

Stalking back into the bathroom, she eyed the shelf of styling products and groaned. None of them worked miracles, but with a little time, Hope knew she could at least tame the curls down to a manageable level. Good thing Ted asked her to come around later on because this could take a while.

An hour later, she was mildly pleased with the results. Next up was organizing the goodies she was planning on bringing to the office and maybe making a little something for her brother for dinner since Hope was certain he hadn't taken the time to eat. There had been no plan on her part to prepare a big dinner for herself, but after a few minutes of scrounging around the kitchen, she was able to throw together a quick chicken pot pie. While it was baking, she set about separating cookies into tins and getting her handy insulated travel bag ready to go.

At seven-thirty on the dot, she texted Ted about her arrival. She was surprised to see her brother waiting for her at the door, his expression grim. "Hey," she said cautiously. "Is this a bad time?"

"No…no," Ted said and looked around uncertainly. "Come on in. Let me just lock this up behind you." Once he was done, he turned around and gave Hope a small smile.

"Seriously, what's going on? If it's not okay for me to be here, I'll just give you the food and go. I don't want to get you in any trouble."

"It's not that," he said and took the bag from her hand. "It's just…well, Jerome was fired."

"What?" she cried. "Why?"

Ted shrugged. "I'm not sure. Something about cutbacks and how the company could save money by hiring an outside security company." He looked at his shoes and then walked slowly toward the elevators. "That way we don't have to pay anything into insurance policies and whatnot."

"That's horrible! And at Christmas?" She snorted with disgust and stomped past her brother when the elevator door opened. "And you wonder why I hate your boss," she murmured.

"Look, I don't particularly agree with it either, but…it's just business."

"What if it were your job that was just eliminated to cut costs right now? How would you feel?"

"I guess…"

"You'd be pissed," she interrupted. "You told me Jerome needed this job–that his wife had health issues. I'm sure your ogre of a boss knows that too." She growled with frustration. "Ooh…I'd like five minutes alone with that man to just…just…punch him in the throat!"

"Easy, Hope," Ted said nervously. "I told you, you have to relax. Especially if you're going to come around here and visit. I can't have you bad-mouthing my boss. Anyone could hear you!"

"Like I care!"

"Well I do!" he snapped. "You know, you don't have to agree with what I do or where I work, but if you're going to come around here, then you have to show a little respect or you're going to have to leave."

Hope stared at him incredulously. "Are you for real right now? I'm here bringing you and your co-workers food and you're threatening to toss me out?"

Ted sighed loudly as the elevator arrived at

their floor. "I'm not threatening you, Hope. Don't be so dramatic. All I'm saying is that you need to just...tone it down while you're here. Please. For me."

She rolled her eyes. This is what she got for trying to do something nice. "Fine. I won't say anything more about the jackass you work for." The doors opened at that moment and she immediately stepped out and began walking toward the kitchen. "I brought you some dinner," she said over her shoulder. "I figured you hadn't eaten. It's nothing major–just some chicken pot pie."

"Really?"

"Yeah. Really." Together they began to pull containers out of the bag. "This big tin is for you to take home."

He smiled. "What did you make this time?"

"Okay, we've got butterscotch blondie bars, brownie thins, traditional chocolate chip cookies, and raspberry chocolate macaroons."

"How do you do it?" he asked reverently as he opened the tin and pulled out a cookie. With his mouth full, he continued, "How do you manage to get all of this baking done and work?"

"Part of the joys of working from home. My oven is only ten feet away at all times. I can work on my web designs while things are baking. And I don't sleep very much."

"You're amazing. You know that, right?"

"Oh stop," she said and pulled the rest of the tins out of the bag. "I had a tin here for Jerome but I guess it will just be extra for your office."

"This is really sweet of you, Hope. I mean it.

You don't even know my co-workers."

She shrugged. "Yeah, but…they have to put up with you so I figured I owed them something sweet," she teased.

"Ha, ha, very funny." Ted put his cookie tin down and glanced at his watch. "Um…I hate to do this to you, but I have a conference call I'm scheduled to be on in five minutes."

"Oh…oh, no big deal," she said and quickly took the dinner she prepared out of the bag and put it in the refrigerator. "That's the pot pie. You can heat it up whenever you're ready."

"Have you eaten?" he asked, concern covering his features.

"Yes," she lied. No need for him to feel bad about throwing her out when she had planned on eating with him. After all, he had no idea she was even bringing the meal. "I just made extra for you." She smiled. "Go. I don't want you to be late. Will there be someone downstairs to let me out?"

Ted nodded. "There should be. If there's not, text me and I'll text security. We have a new system now."

"Okay. Thanks." Walking toward him, she got on her tiptoes and kissed Ted's cheek. "Eat some of the real food and not just the cookies."

"I make no promises," he said with a lopsided grin and walked out of the kitchen. "Thanks again, Hope. Are we still on for Saturday?"

She nodded. "Wouldn't miss it." Although, truth be told, she felt slightly deflated at the moment and the thought of coming back here was a little less appealing. Jerome was gone. Beckett wasn't around and she had put all this effort into looking slightly attractive for nothing. "Well damn," she mumbled and looked around the kitchen to make sure she hadn't forgotten anything.

"Another drive-by dinner?" a deep male voice said from behind her.

Stunned, Hope quickly turned around and smiled. "Beckett! Hey! How are you?" *Down girl.* Don't sound so anxious.

"Good," he said, a smile on his face. "Where's your brother?"

"What? Oh, he had a conference call and I didn't know. I made him dinner and brought him some more cookies. Different variety this time. And I made extras for his co-workers. I just hope he doesn't eat them all before tomorrow."

With a chuckle, Beckett stepped into the kitchen. "Well if he does, I can't say that I blame him."

"Really?"

"Fishing for compliments?"

"Maybe," she blushed.

Beckett leaned in close. "They were delicious. I'm embarrassed to say that I ate them all."

"Well…today could be your lucky day. If you're interested."

One dark brow arched as he took a small step back.

"I…I had brought another tin to try to give to Jerome," she paused, "but Ted tells me he's been let go. So, if you'd like, I have this extra batch of cookies." As soon as the words were out of her mouth, she wanted to call them back. Hope remembered Beckett's reaction the last time she offered him the cookies and the thought of him hesitating again was almost painful. "I mean…"

"I'd love them. Thanks." His smile was big and he reached out and took the tin for himself, not even waiting for Hope to hand them over.

She mentally sighed with relief. "Like I said, they're all different this time. I tend to subscribe to the twenty-five days of Christmas cookies philosophy."

"Twenty-five? That's a lot of baking," he chuckled.

She nodded. "I got a late start this year so it will be more like the twelve days of Christmas cookies."

"Well, as long as you're at least sticking to the Christmas theme," he teased.

Another nod. "I try. Although, I should probably just stop. It seems I'm only baking for Ted and his co-workers. And you," she added with a smile.

"I'm sure there are plenty of people who would love for you to share them."

"It's more out of habit or tradition that I do it. My mom and I used to bake like this every year because we always had a huge party on Christmas Eve. This is the first year ever that it's not happening." Emotion started to clog her throat and she tried to calm herself before speaking again. "Anyway, old habits die hard."

He gave her a sympathetic smile. "This year will be hard but I'm sure as time goes on, you'll find a way to pass on the tradition and make it your own. Find your own people to celebrate with."

"Maybe. I just wish that this year didn't suck so much."

They were quiet for several moments. "So what was tonight's dinner?" he asked.

"Oh, nothing major. A chicken pot pie. I guess I should have checked with Ted before I went through the trouble. I thought we'd eat it together but, like I said, he had a call to get to."

"So you didn't eat?"

Hope shook her head. "It's not a big deal. I'll grab something on the way home and eat in front of the TV."

"Sounds exciting," he said with a grin.

"Oh, you have no idea. There's no way I'm going to go home and cook after, technically, I already did."

"Why don't you just take the pot pie home with you and eat it yourself?"

She looked at him like he was crazy. "Because I already brought it here for Ted. And told him about it. And showed him where it is in the refrigerator," she laughed. "That would be terribly rude of me to just take it back."

He shrugged. "Not really. You already cooked for him on Saturday and baked him a ton of cookies. Seems to me like you spoil him."

"Well, he's all that I have," she said simply.

"I find that very hard to believe. Surely you have friends? A boyfriend?"

Interesting, she thought. "Friends, yes. Boyfriend, no. I'm afraid I'm a bit of a workaholic myself and because I work from home, I don't go out very much."

Beckett's dark eyes studied her for a long moment. He was still holding the tin of cookies in his hands. "Listen, I…um, I have to run down to my office for a minute but maybe we can grab something to eat."

Hope's eyes went wide. "Together?"

He nodded. "Yeah, together."

"Oh…um…"

"Unless you'd rather not," he said quickly. "I mean, if you'd really prefer just doing the drive-thru thing and going home, I'd completely understand and…"

"Beckett?"

"Yeah?"

"I'd really like to have dinner with you."

His shoulders seemed to relax. He nodded. "Good. That's good." Glancing at his watch, he looked back up at Hope. "Can I meet you down in the lobby in ten minutes?"

"Absolutely," she said with a smile of her own. "I'll see you downstairs."

"I have to admit, I never knew there were twenty-five different varieties of Christmas cookies," Beckett said thirty minutes later as they sat across from each other at a small diner close to the office.

"I think there's more than that. These are just my personal favorites."

"You have excellent taste then."

"Thanks." She smiled and Hope sat there in a bit of a giddy haze. Beckett was handsome, intelligent and a great conversationalist. How did she get this lucky? She hadn't been on a date in almost a year and all it took was a visit to her brother's office for her to meet a great guy? Ted was definitely getting a mountain of cookies this weekend.

"So tell me about your business," he said and smiled warmly at her.

"Well, I'm a total computer geek," she said with a chuckle. "I play video games and love figuring out how to program things. I know most people think of it as a guy thing, but I figured out a long time ago that I had a knack for it." She stopped and took a sip of her sweet tea. "I didn't think I'd be able to make a decent living at it, especially working only for myself, but I lucked out with some local businesses and had a couple of friends who knew people and it just took off."

"Did you want to work for yourself? Wouldn't it have been more lucrative for you to go to work for somebody else? There'd be a little more stability in that, I would imagine."

"It's possible. And actually I did start out working for someone else but the kind of work they were giving me was almost insulting. I was the only woman in the office and after a while I noticed how I was getting the really small jobs or the ones that any first-year graphic design student could do. When I approached my boss about it, he essentially told me I could take it or leave it. I chose to leave it."

"That had to be scary–just walking out and starting your own business."

Hope shrugged. "I didn't need a whole lot for start-up costs. I already had a couple of computers and I hit up some friends first and then started combing the community for potential clients. Some were one-time gigs and others turned into long term projects."

"How many clients do you have now?"

Taking a minute to do the calculation, she said, "I have about a dozen steady clients. Most of them have me doing monthly updates on their websites; others have me doing the artwork for their promotional materials."

"Artwork? So you're an artist too?" he asked with just a hint of surprise.

She nodded. "That's really how it all started. Back in high school I loved to draw comics. Superheroes and cartoon characters, that sort of thing. I always loved video games and I guess I really got hooked when I tried to find a way to merge the two."

Beckett chuckled and shook his head. "I know it's not funny but I'm having a hard time sitting here picturing you playing video games. I mean, I guess I could see you doing those puzzle type of games but certainly nothing like the popular shooter games or anything like that."

Hope arched a brow at him. "Oh really? Do you play? The shooter games?"

"As a matter of fact I do. Occasionally."

"Well, we just might have to see who's better some time."

A look of surprise crossed his face. "Like a challenge?"

She nodded. "Oh yeah. What system do you have?"

"Xbox One and a PlayStation Four."

"Very nice," she said approvingly.

"And you?"

"Same."

"Interesting."

Their meals were served and they ate in silence for a few minutes. "So how about you?" Hope asked. "What do you do with James Enterprises?"

Beckett waved her off. "Nothing as exciting as graphic design and drawing comic books."

"Now I think you're making fun of me," she said with a smirk.

"Me? No," he said playfully. "Tell me, do you go to Comic-Con?"

Hope blushed and couldn't force herself to make direct eye contact. "Maybe."

He chuckled. "That's a yes and it probably means you dress up for it too."

"Weren't we talking about you?" she asked, desperate to change the subject.

"I'm sorry. Just the image of you dressed up as Wonder Woman is stuck in my mind."

"Please...Wonder Woman is way too obvious. And overdone." She took another sip of her drink. "And you still haven't told me about your job."

"In a minute," he said, placing his elbows on the table as he leaned in close to her. "You can't just leave it at that. The curiosity is killing me!"

Hope let out a loud and dramatic sigh. "Okay.

Fine. But if I tell you, you have to quit stalling and answer my question."

"Whatever you want," he said with a big grin and a twinkle in his eyes.

Sitting up a little straighter in her seat, Hope braced herself to reveal her nerdy hobby. "I've only gone to three conventions…"

"Quit stalling."

She frowned at him. "The first year I went as Poison Ivy, the next I went as Mystique and last year I went as…" God this was embarrassing. "Princess Leia."

"Please tell me it was the gold bikini," he begged as he leaned even closer to her. Hope nodded and he groaned.

"Okay, now that I've thoroughly embarrassed myself, it's your turn."

"There's no way I can top that."

"Quit stalling," she said, mimicking his earlier taunt.

"Actually, I do a lot of research and development. I find locations for new sites as well as find resorts that are struggling and figure out the profitability in going in and buying them out and making them part of the James company."

"Wow!" she said, her eyes going wide. "That sounds very impressive."

He shrugged. "It certainly keeps me busy."

"I would imagine. How many people are in your department?"

Beckett took a sip of his soda before answering. "I don't even know. It seems to change all the time. I don't even focus on that. I'm usually too busy in my own office to pay attention to the revolving door of employees."

That sounded a little harsh to Hope but she chose to keep her mouth shut. "Okay then...so, what are your plans for Christmas? Anything exciting? Traveling?"

He shook his head. "Work. I don't really do anything for Christmas."

Hope wasn't sure what to make of that. Did that mean he didn't celebrate Christmas for religious beliefs or personal ones? Was there a tactful way to ask? "Oh. Do you...um...do you have family close by?"

Beckett shook his head again. "No."

Way to be vague, she thought to herself. "No, you don't have any relatives or no, they don't live close by?" He looked over at her with what Hope could only describe as annoyance and she immediately regretted asking for clarification. "You know what...never mind. It doesn't matter," she said quickly and focused on finishing her burger.

The silence was palpable and it wasn't until the waitress came and cleared their dishes away before Beckett finally spoke. "I have a brother and a sister. We don't really speak." He finished his soda. "Our parents died about eight years ago–actually, our mother died when we were young and our father died eight years ago. There were a lot of...disagreements, shall we say, over the estate. We haven't spoken since."

"That's kind of sad. Don't you miss them?" Immediately she wanted to kick herself for asking such a personal question.

"No. I believe it's best for all of us if we don't talk," he said simply. "What about you and your brother? Ted, right? Are you close?"

"Oh yeah. And not because we just lost our parents. We've always been close. We're only a year apart in age and we were both always kind of geeky so we bonded over our mutual interests."

"Interesting. And does he have an artistic side like you?"

Hope laughed out loud. "Absolutely not! And believe me when I say that I absolutely loathe math."

"Isn't math at least partially involved in graphic design?"

"A little. But I could never work with numbers to the degree that Ted does. My brain would go numb."

That had him laughing. "I can relate. It certainly takes a special kind of person to be able to keep all of those numbers straight." He looked like he was about to say more when his cell phone rang. "Excuse me for a moment," he said before standing and walking away to take the call.

For the most part, Hope couldn't really gauge how the evening was going. Beckett seemed to get annoyed easily when asked anything too personal and he also seemed to a have a little bit of a weird outlook on his job and his co-workers. Hope wasn't big on working in an office either, but at least when she did she had basic common decency toward the people she worked with.

Maybe she was wrong about him.

He was definitely attractive and had a lot of marks in the "pros" column she had mentally created, but the "cons" column was quickly catching up. Still, she wouldn't regret taking the risk and going out with him tonight. It was a pleasant distraction, if nothing else, and made her realize how lucky she was that she still had Ted in her life. How sad it must be to have family you dislike so much that you'd rather not even speak to them.

"Hope...I'm really sorry," Beckett said as he came back to the table and waved the waitress over. "But I have to go. There's a problem with a real estate deal we're working on and I have to head back to the office."

She looked at her watch. "At this hour?"

He chuckled. "I know. You wouldn't think that real estate deals were something that would go on at all hours of the day and night, but they do. I thought someone else was handling the negotiations but they've hit a snag and now it's time for me to step in."

"I understand. Don't worry about it." They had driven to the diner together in Beckett's SUV, so she knew they were going to have to get going quickly. She watched him pay the check and then waited for her to stand and join him. Like a gentleman, he helped Hope with her jacket and then held the door for her as they exited the diner.

"I'm sorry I had to cut our time short. You didn't even get to order dessert." He sounded genuinely remorseful and as he helped Hope into the car, he leaned in close, his gaze intense. "I promise to make it up to you next time."

A little shiver of delight danced down her spine. Beckett may not be the perfect man, but she certainly wouldn't mind a second date.

∾ུ∾

By Saturday, Hope was beginning to feel like she had seriously misjudged things. After Beckett had dropped her off back at her car on Wednesday night, she gave him her phone number and he promised to call.

But he didn't.

She tried not to let it get to her but as she was driving back over to James Enterprises to have dinner with Ted and Merry, she couldn't help but feel a little apprehensive. What would happen if she saw him? Could she possibly pull off looking and feeling casual when inside she was screaming *"Why haven't you called?"*

Not likely.

The only thing saving her was that Merry had volunteered to bring dinner and dessert so there was absolutely no chance of Hope offering anything to Beckett should she run into him and try to lure him into conversation.

Where had she gone wrong? She thought for the millionth time in days. They seemed to have a good time and Beckett had definitely seemed interested in her. Okay, maybe she had simply misread his intentions. Or feelings. Or whatever. He certainly hadn't tried to kiss her when they had arrived back at the parking garage and he dropped her at her car. Actually, he had been seriously distracted so Hope had made a hasty retreat after thanking him for dinner. It wasn't until she was unlocking her car door that Beckett had rolled down his window and asked for her phone number.

None of this was new information. She had been reviewing the mental tape running in her head ever since and she was still no closer to figuring out why he hadn't called. And then she cursed herself–again–for being one of those women who obsessed over why a guy didn't call and she vowed right then and there to just…stop.

"No more," she muttered as she pulled into a parking spot. Taking a deep breath, Hope pulled out her phone and texted her brother. He immediately wrote back asking her to wait for Merry so they could just walk in together. It made sense but Merry had a tendency never to be on time and Hope didn't want to sit out in her car all by herself while she waited. "Fine."

Luckily she didn't have to wait too long. Merry's little white Smart car pulled in beside her and Hope had to sigh. It wasn't that she didn't like Merry, it was just…Merry tended to be a tad…boring. She was super practical, like she always seemed to be doing whatever was the safest, the most predictable…the most vanilla. For the life of her, Hope didn't understand what her brother saw in Merry but whatever it was, he obviously loved it.

"Hey!" she said cheerily, climbing out of the car and facing her soon-to-be sister-in-law. "Can I help you with anything?"

"Oh, no. But thank you. I have everything

contained in this insulated bag. I was going to bring dessert but it wouldn't fit." Merry Williams pushed her black rimmed glasses up on her nose and turned to lock her car. She was dressed in her scrubs and her hair was pulled back in a sensible ponytail–and she wore no makeup.

Another sigh escaped before Hope could stop it.

"Is something wrong, Hope? Are you feeling okay?" Merry asked with concern.

"What? No, no, I'm fine," she said quickly. What else could she say? *Hey, how about putting a little effort into your appearance for my brother, huh?* Um…not likely. Although, maybe Merry had the right idea. The last time Hope put in an effort in hopes of impressing a man it resulted in…*Stop it*! No more thoughts about Beckett and his no calling ways.

Or his sexy black hair and dark eyes.

Dammit.

"I made macaroni and cheese. It's one of Ted's favorites," Merry said as they walked to the front entrance.

Hope texted Ted to let him know they were ready to come in and hoped that someone was available to open the doors. Merry continued to ramble on about some of Ted's favorite meals and Hope didn't have the heart to tell her how most of them were incorrect. Either Ted was out and out lying to his fiancée or poor Merry just wasn't very attentive. Either way, Hope resigned herself to a perfectly boring meal.

And no dessert.

A uniformed security guard let them in and checked their IDs before letting them go up in the elevator. Once the door was closed, Hope looked over at Merry. "Have you ever been here before?"

"No."

Okay. Let's try that again. "I was hoping there would be more people working late with Ted, but both times I've come here like this, it's just been him. I kind of feel bad for him."

"Hmm."

Hope rolled her eyes and decided to finish the ride in silence. The doors opened on the eleventh floor and Hope led the way to the kitchen. Once there, she decided to let Merry do her thing while she texted her brother that they were waiting for him. With nothing to do, Hope wandered out into the hallway and did her best not to snoop around in hopes of seeing Beckett. While they had talked about his job, he never quite said where in the building he actually worked.

Before her curiosity got the better of her, she spotted a frazzled-looking Ted heading her way. "Hey, is everything all right?" she asked when he was beside her.

His hair was sticking out all over the place and he definitely looked tense. "I…it's fine. It's fine. Does Merry have everything ready? I'm afraid I don't have a lot of time tonight."

"Again?" Hope asked and then felt like she kicked a puppy when Ted turned to her. "I'm sorry. That was uncalled for. What does Mr. James have you doing now?"

"It doesn't matter." They walked into the

kitchen and Ted immediately sat down without even greeting Merry.

Hope stood back in fascination as she watched the two of them interact with one another–Merry placed Ted's plate of food down in front of him and handed him a napkin. Then she went about setting out the other two plates before silently sitting down beside Ted. He poured their drinks and they both started eating before she even sat down.

Yawn.

"So," she said brightly, pulling up a chair and sitting down, "macaroni and cheese! Yum!"

Both Ted and Merry nodded but didn't look up from their plates.

"I can't remember the last time I made it from scratch myself," she said, pushing her portion around on her plate because it did not look appetizing at all. "I'm more of the box mix with the powder kind of girl. Three for a dollar!"

They both nodded again without looking up.

Worst. Dinner. Ever.

Deciding to wave the white flag, Hope managed to choke down a couple of bites before her stomach threatened to rebel. If this was one of Ted's favorites, she hated to think of the meals he flat out rejected. This was beyond horrible. It was dry and the pasta was undercooked, but the silence was far worse than the food. Hope spent a large part of her days with no one to talk to because she worked alone so there was no way she was going to sit with two other people in silence.

"So, Merry, Ted tells me you're working the Christmas shift in the ER. Will you get to be at home at all for Christmas?"

Merry shook her head and gently placed her fork down before reaching for a napkin and dabbing the corners of her mouth. "I took a double," she said finally. "I'll sleep in the on-call room. Since Ted is going to be out of town and my family lives so far away, it seemed pointless to be at home."

Hope wasn't sure why. With the long hours Ted normally worked, what would be the difference? "And Ted," she said, facing her brother, "when do you leave to go and work with your boss?"

"We'll be heading out of town Wednesday," he said quietly.

"Wednesday?" Hope cried. "But...but that's six days before Christmas! Why do you have to leave so early? I mean, isn't it bad enough that you're missing the actual holiday? He can't even let you have maybe a small pre-Christmas dinner with your fiancée? Your sister?"

"Hope," he warned.

"No, I'm serious," she said and stood up abruptly. "It's not right, Ted! Are you being compensated for all of this extra time and inconvenience? Are you getting overtime pay? Holiday pay?"

"It's not like that," he began.

"Then what would you call it? Do you think you're going to work a normal shift while you're at this guy's house? And why do you even have to go to his house? Does he have family he's planning on spending Christmas with while you're there slaving away for him? Is that it?"

"As far as I know, Mr. James doesn't have any family. It will just be the two of us working. We've got several new resorts planned for next year as well as three expansions. There's a lot to get done and if we can buckle down over the holidays and get it all done, we'll be ahead of schedule after New Year's."

Something in the way he said it had Hope on alert. "Are you saying you'll be gone for New Year's too?"

He nodded solemnly.

Hope looked over at Merry in hopes of getting a little back up in the outrage department and wanted to scream when the woman continued to eat. "Merry? Aren't you the least bit upset that Ted is going to be gone for so long? That's two weeks!"

Merry looked up at Hope with confusion. "It's his job, Hope. Obviously, Mr. James must think very highly of Ted if he's willing to work with him one-on-one over the holidays to meet this deadline."

"But there is no deadline!" Hope yelled. "Ted, you just said that by working through the holidays you'd be ahead of schedule. Why can't you just work like normal people who get the holidays off and finish on time?"

Ted sighed with frustration and pushed his own plate away. "I can't keep arguing with you like this, Hope," he snapped. "I thought the three of us could at least have a nice dinner together here tonight, but clearly I was mistaken. I think you should leave."

Seriously? He was kicking her out? The nerve! "Fine, you know what? That's just…fine. Whatever." Snapping up her jacket and purse, she stormed from the kitchen and down the hall to the elevator.

The man had nerve! She'd baked him cookies and brought him dinner–that was edible!–and she was the one who got kicked out? Well fine. Let them finish their perfectly boring little meal of crunchy macaroni and cheese all by themselves. There was a Chinese takeout place on her way home that would *love* her company!

Hope paced in the elevator and stormed across the lobby with the single-minded intent of just getting the hell out of Dodge. At the front door, she found it locked and slammed on the door. "Dammit!" Whirling around, she tried to see if the security guard was nearby. "Hey! Anyone around? I need to get out of here!"

No answer.

"I hate this place. I hate this place. I hate this place." She paced back and forth and then said, "Screw it" and unlocked the door and walked out. No alarms sounded and no one came running after her. Not that it mattered. She'd pretty much tell them to take a hike and keep walking if they tried to catch her.

By the time she was back at her car, she was beyond fuming. Needing to vent a little, she walked over to Merry's car and kicked a tire. "*Ow!* Stupid car. Stupid practical, boring car! You suck and your macaroni and cheese sucks and I hope you both choke on it!"

"I didn't know cars could make macaroni and cheese."

Hope turned around and found Beckett

standing next to her car. She was not in the mood for jokes and just glared at him.

"I know they're called Smart cars but if they created one that could cook, I might be tempted to buy it."

Ignoring him, she stormed around the front of her car to the driver's side door and unlocked it.

"Hey, are you all right?" he asked, walking over and putting a hand on her arm.

Hope swiftly pulled away. "You know what? No. I'm not all right. I'm tired, I'm pissed off, I just ate the world's worst dinner and now my toe hurts. So no, Beckett. I'm not all right." She yanked the door open and tossed her purse inside. She was just about to climb in when he stopped her. Her eyes shot up to his.

"You're obviously upset. Please, tell me what's wrong?"

Leaning back against the car frame, she glared at him for a minute. She had been so annoyed with Ted and Merry that she had forgotten she was annoyed with him too. It was on the tip of her tongue to just completely unload on him, but she decided against it. "It's…it's nothing. Really. I just need to go."

"Hope," he said softly and took a step closer. "Come on. You can talk to me."

Could she? Right now it didn't seem like such a good idea. "Look, I appreciate your concern but…it's just been a bad night."

"What happened?"

Where could she even begin?

When she remained silent, Beckett seemed to

take the hint. "Okay," he said with a small smile. "Will you be having dinner with your brother again this week?"

And just like that, she snapped. "Um...that would be a big fat no. Why? Because thanks to his jackass of a boss, he's leaving on Wednesday to go out of town and won't be back until after New Year's. So that means that the world's worst macaroni and cheese was my Christmas dinner with my brother. That's it. Bad, crunchy, undercooked, dry mac and cheese. Banner holiday for me!" she added sarcastically. "And then, as if the food wasn't bad enough, he threw me out!"

"What? Why would he do that?"

"You want to know why?" Hope was on a roll now. "It's this place. There is something about this...this...place," she spat, "that just brings out the worst in me. I can't even explain it. I just come here and it makes me mad!"

"You can't blame the building for ruining your dinner," he said logically.

"No, I blame the dinner for ruining dinner," she said, "but I just...I just can't come back here anymore."

"I don't understand."

Hope rolled her eyes. "What does this James guy do? Does he brainwash all of you? Is that it?"

"What...?"

"You all seem to be overworked, underpaid, you have to work holidays and on top of that, he fired Jerome!"

"Who?"

"The security guard. Older guy. Worked here

until about a week ago? Any of this ringing a bell?" At that moment, Hope wasn't really sure why she was getting so snippy with him, but in all fairness, he wanted to know what was bothering her.

He gave a curt nod. "And this upsets you?"

"Yes it upsets me! I hate seeing people treated unfairly! I hate that the one time of year when I desperately need my brother, he isn't going to be there and I'm going to be all alone! You may not mind not being around your family, but it bothers me!" She felt tears starting to well in her eyes and quickly turned away.

"Isn't there anyone else you could spend Christmas with?" he asked quietly. "Some friends maybe?"

The thought had been swirling around in her head ever since Ted broke the news to her of his newfound holiday work schedule. It wouldn't be the worst thing in the world but Hope wasn't sure how to go about inviting herself to someone's house for Christmas. "I don't know," she muttered. "Maybe." She needed to leave, to get out of here before she did something completely stupid like ask Beckett to spend Christmas with her.

Or hug her.

Not a good thing.

He stood there in front of her, looking all kinds of handsome. His dark hair slightly mussed, a gray wool scarf around his neck and a black wool jacket covering his muscular build. It wasn't fair that he could look so good all the damn time, so calm and completely in control, when her life was spinning in the complete opposite direction.

"I…I really need to go," she said finally and then forced herself to look up and meet his eyes. Damn. They were so dark, so intense and it would be so easy to just look into them forever. A sigh escaped before she could stop it. "Merry Christmas, Beckett," she said with a bit of a forced smile.

"You too, Hope."

"And I guess a Happy New Year, too," she added and turned to climb into her car when his hand on her arm stopped her again. It was on the tip of her tongue to ask what he wanted, but suddenly his lips were on hers and Hope had to remember how to breathe.

His lips were gentle at first but once she seemed to overcome her shock and relax, Beckett's hands came up and cupped her face, caressed her cheeks. Hope sighed as her own hands crept up and clutched the front of his coat. It was so unexpected, such a complete surprise to her that she needed to keep herself anchored to something or her knees would surely give out and she'd be in a puddle on the ground.

After Beckett seemed satisfied with introducing himself to her through his kiss, he deepened it. His hand traveled up and into the riotous curls on her head as he moved closer to her. The feel of his lean body pressed up against hers sent Hope's own into overdrive. Over and over he slanted his lips over hers, his tongue teased hers, his breath mingled with hers. It was glorious and all-consuming and yet all she could do was purr against him.

Long moments later when Beckett finally lifted his head from hers, he stared down into her face.

"Happy New Year, Hope," he said, his voice slightly rough and gravelly. His hand trailed down her cheek to her chin before he let her go and stepped back.

And walked away.

Chapter Three

On Wednesday afternoon, Hope was on the road to Tennessee. Deciding to drop out of her self-imposed pity-party, she called her college roommate Tara, and managed an invitation to come to Knoxville for the holidays. It wasn't a horrible plan but it still wasn't what Hope wanted most for Christmas.

She wanted to have her family together.

Although, if she were completely honest with herself, she was never going to have that again. It was pointless to hold on to a dream that was never going to be a reality. Now there was a depressing thought. Deciding to let it go, a quick scan through the radio stations had her finding the one that only played Christmas music.

For a hundred miles, Hope sang off-key to some of her favorite holiday songs and actually started to feel better about her circumstances. It was obvious that Ted was not going to be the family support she longed for. The more she thought about it, the more Hope realized the closeness she and her brother shared had slowly faded away over the years. They just didn't notice it because they were busy with their own lives and still had their parents around to bring them back every once in a while.

"And we're back to depressed," she sighed as the miles of highway kept going by. The sky was gray and the temperatures weren't favorable. With any luck, she'd be through the mountains and across the North Carolina-Tennessee line before anything changed or worsened. The last thing she needed was to have to do this drive in the snow. As it was, she had chosen to leave so many days before Christmas to avoid as much traffic as possible. With a hotel reservation waiting for her over the state line, even if it did start to snow, Hope was confident she'd have a place to rest for the night and not have to rush to get to Tara's.

An hour later, her cell phone rang and she looked at it as if it were a foreign object. All of her clients knew of her travel plans and it was rare for her to get social calls. She tapped the screen on her dashboard and saw it was Merry.

And groaned.

It was highly unusual for Merry to call her, especially in the middle of the day, so Hope's curiosity got the better of her and she answered. "Hey, Merry!" she said with a cheeriness she did not feel. "What can I do for you?"

"Hope? Hope, can you hear me?" Merry's voice was shaky and she sounded a little bit…off.

Hope was instantly alarmed.

"Merry? What's the matter? What's going on?"

"Hope, I can't get Ted on the phone." Her voice faded out and she coughed a few times before speaking again. "I…I don't know how to get in touch with him. Do you have another number for him?"

"Unfortunately, I don't. Why? What's happened? Are you all right?"

"I had an accident," she sobbed. "My car is a mess and…and…I'm in so much pain."

"Are you at the hospital? Merry, please tell me you're at the hospital!"

"I…I'm waiting for the ambulance. I'm scared, Hope. I need Ted. Please! You have to get in touch with Ted!"

"Okay, okay…I haven't talked to him since we had dinner Saturday night. I don't know where exactly he was going. I'll keep calling him."

"No!" Merry cried. "You have to find out where he is! You have to get him to come home. Please, Hope. Please! I need him here with me!"

Hope was able to hear the sound of an ambulance siren in the background. "Merry, I want you to listen to me. I want you to hang up and let the paramedics take care of you."

"But…but…Ted! I need Ted! Promise me! Promise me, Hope, you're going to find him and get him here!"

"I promise. I'm going to hang up and find him right now and get him to you as soon as possible. Okay?"

"Thank you. Thank you, Hope!" Merry cried and then the line went dead.

The only problem with her promise was the fact that Hope was driving down I-40 and had no idea where her brother was. Ted had mentioned how G.B. James' place was in the mountains but…what mountains? Where? "This is a nightmare." Eyes back on the road, Hope waited until she saw a sign for a rest area and pulled over. If she was going to have to search and make calls to find out where exactly Ted was, she needed to be off the road to do it.

"Good thing I'm not in a rush," she said to herself as she pulled into a large parking lot and found a place to park. "Okay, where to start?" The obvious choice was with Ted himself. She called and the phone went directly to voicemail. That usually meant his phone was off so texting him would be of no use. Next was to call his office. It was true that he was supposed to be leaving today to head out of town, but that didn't mean he'd already left or that someone there couldn't reach him.

"James Enterprises. How may I direct your call?" the operator asked.

Good question. "Yes, um…hi. This is Hope Cooper. My brother Ted works up on the eleventh floor…something with…financing." She cursed herself. What kind of person didn't know what department their brother worked in? "It's very important that I reach him. Can you…?"

"Hold please."

"Dammit!" The world's worst music immediately began to play and Hope prayed someone would answer soon.

"You've reached the desk of Theodore Cooper. I'll be away from my desk until after January second. Please direct all your inquiries to…"

Hope quickly reached into her purse and found a piece of paper and pen and wrote down the number just in case she got disconnected. Luckily, with a quick press of the number five, her call was being transferred.

More bad music.

"This is Diane Charles, how may I help you?"

Oh, thank God, Hope sighed. "Hi. Diane. Um…this is Hope Cooper. Ted's sister. I was wondering…"

"Oh, Hope! We absolutely loved your cookies. Thank you so much! I have to say, I was never one for baking so I always either bought store-made cookies or got one of those cookie dough logs where you just cut and throw them on a baking sheet!" She laughed. "Sometimes I would just eat the dough raw! I know you're not supposed to but, hey, who are we kidding? It's delicious! Am I right?"

"Diane…"

"Those brownie thins were to die for! Honestly, I thought I would die if we ran out of them!" She laughed again. "Don't tell Ted but…I went and took the rest of them and hid them in my drawer! I am just about out of them so if you have any extras you want to share, feel free to send them my way!"

"Yeah, yeah…I'll see. Listen, I need to…"

"Do you bake them all from scratch or are

some of them from a box mix? I mean, there's nothing wrong with a box mix. My mom uses them for all of our baking but I would imagine for all the great things you bake, it's probably something more than that. Right? Is there a trick to getting the right ingredients? You know, are there better brands of flour to use? Or a certain type of baking pan that's better than others? I was thinking…"

"*Diane!*" Hope snapped, her patience gone. "I promise I will make you a hundred brownie thins for the New Year if you can just help me for a minute. Okay?"

"Um…sure," she said hesitantly.

"I can't get Ted on the phone. Actually, I think his phone is off. Is he in the office today by chance?"

"No. He and Mr. James left already."

"Okay. Great. Do you have a way to reach them?"

"You mean by phone?"

Seriously? This woman was in the finance department and she was asking these kinds of questions? "Um…yeah. Or any other way we can reach them actually. There's an emergency. Ted's fiancée…"

"Merry?"

"Yes, yes. Merry. She's been in an accident. She drives one of those Smart cars. They're very small and she says it's totaled."

"Oh, my…"

"When I hung up with her, the paramedics were just arriving. It's very important I get in touch with Ted. Please. Can you help me?"

Diane was silent for a moment. "Mr. James said not to bother them unless it was important."

"And this clearly is," Hope prompted.

"Let me get your number, Hope, and I'll try to get them on the phone and one of us will get back to you."

"Thank you! Thank you, Diane! And believe me, I will get those brownie thins to you after the holidays. You have my word." Hope gave her the phone number, hung up and prepared to wait. As much as she wasn't a fan of Merry's, she certainly didn't wish the woman any harm. Hopefully, Diane would be able to reach Ted and he'd be able to go and comfort his fiancée and then meet up with his boss later.

Or not at all.

And wouldn't that just solve everyone's problems?

Well, not Mr. James', but that didn't really matter to Hope. As far she was concerned, Mr. G.B. James could go to hell. Ha! The only thing that would make that statement feel even better was if she ever had the opportunity to tell him so to his stupid face! Yeah, that's right. Stupid. Face. Hey, every once in a while her inner twelve-year-old needed to come out and play. "Sue me," she grumbled and stared at the phone in hand.

"Come on, Ted," she said, as if willing the phone to hear her. "Just call me so I can relay the message and get back on the road. I'll be quick, I promise."

Ten minutes later, her phone was still silent. To pass the time, Hope climbed out of the car and

65

walked into the rest area pavilion and to search for a vending machine. Nothing helped pass the time like a candy bar or a bag of pretzels. Sizing up her options, she eventually made her selection and walked back out to her car.

"Well that killed all of five minutes," she murmured. And cursed. "Who goes away and doesn't leave a way for people to reach them?" Just then her phone rang. It was Ted's office. "Hello?"

"Hi, Hope. It's Diane."

"Any luck?"

"Unfortunately no," she sighed. "Neither of them are answering their phones. I left messages for both of them and even called Mr. James' emergency service and left a message with them just in case he called in. I just don't know what else to do."

Hope had a plan. It wasn't even a Plan B. More like Plan W. "Do you know where Mr. James' home?"

"The Lodge? Well sure! But it's a long way from here. I'd hate for you to drive all the way out there and have them finally check their messages."

"No worries," Hope sighed. "I'm already on the road and heading west toward Tennessee."

"Well that's convenient!" Diane said excitedly. "You're heading their way!"

"Really? Where? Where is his home?"

"Oh it's not just a home, Hope. It's a lodge. An honest to goodness ski lodge. The only problem is it's no longer a running lodge. Mr. James just uses it as a private home now. Rumor has it it was an amazing place when it was open to the public, a real swanky place to stay."

If it were possible, Hope would reach through the phone and strangle this woman. Why couldn't she focus on what was important here? "And where is this…swanky lodge, Diane?" she asked patiently.

"Oh, right…it's right outside of Sugar Mountain."

That literally meant nothing to Hope. "I have no idea where that is."

"It's north of Asheville. If you're driving on I-40, you'll hit Asheville and Sugar Mountain is just north of there. If you'd like, I can text you the address and then you can use your GPS or something to get the directions. Mr. James doesn't like us giving out that kind of information, but under the circumstances…" she began hesitantly.

"He won't hear it from me that you gave me the address, Diane," Hope assured her.

"Thank you," she sighed with relief. "I really like my job and don't want to do anything to lose it. What will you tell him when he asks how you found them?"

"I'm a computer whiz. I'll tell him I did a little internet research and found his address. Don't worry. I can't thank you enough, Diane. Do you happen to know when they got on the road?"

"Hmm…I'd say about two hours ago. I don't know where you are but hopefully they'll get there first."

"That's what I'm hoping for." With a look out the windshield, Hope saw the first few flakes starting to fall. Dammit! "Listen, Diane, I really need to go. If you can text me the address, I would really appreciate it."

"I will. I will. And Hope?"

"Yeah?"

"Tell Ted to please let me know if there's anything we can do for him."

"Thanks. I will." Hanging up, Hope waited for the address to come through via text before she felt comfortable leaving the parking lot. This was so not how she imagined her day going. It had been a long time since she'd taken a road trip and, if she were being honest, Hope would have to say that she was looking forward to it.

"Okay, don't look at this as a bad thing," she said out loud, "think of it as just a detour–a minor extension of your perfectly mapped out road trip." That didn't sound bitter at all, did it?

Five minutes later she had the address plugged into her navigation system and was on the road again. As she drove, several things occurred to her: first, she and Ted never really fought. Ted asking her to leave the office Saturday night was the first time something like that had ever happened. She had no idea how she was supposed to respond when she saw him. Was she still supposed to be upset? Outraged? Or was she supposed to pretend like it never happened?

Second, this would be the first time she was going to meet the big, bad G.B. James. For some reason, she had always been curious about the man but never enough to actually do any homework or research on him. "With all the time I spend on the computer, you'd think I would have Googled the man." Too late for that now. In about two hours she'd be seeing him in person.

Oh, joy.

Hope couldn't quite put her finger on it, but there was just something about the man that rubbed her the wrong way. No, that wasn't quite true; she knew exactly what it was. He was arrogant, overbearing and treated his employees like crap, no matter how much they denied it.

How was it even possible? How was she the only one to see it? If you were to listen to Ted or even to Beckett, the all-mighty G.B. James was a great guy to work for. Again, *how*? They all seemed overworked, had no personal lives and the man made unreasonable demands on them and their time! How could everyone turn a blind eye to it except for her?

It was kind of easy to understand Ted's perspective; he wanted to secure his position within the company so when he married Merry, he'd have a little bit of security. The only problem was that it seemed as if it wouldn't take much to lose that precarious perch on job security and find yourself unemployed. Case in point, Jerome. Poor, sweet Jerome. Hope couldn't quite pinpoint why she kept fixating on the security guard; he was just a nice man, working to take care of his wife and then one day...*BAM*! Unemployed. And for what? The all-mighty dollar.

Like G.B. James didn't have enough of them! The man owned resorts all over the world! Seriously? He couldn't let one man hold onto his job? His dignity? "Oh, crap!" Looking down at her dashboard, Hope saw she was doing well over eighty down the interstate thanks to being so focused on why she hated Ted's boss rather than the road. "Focus. You'll get to meet the man soon enough. And maybe, just maybe...say some of the things that are on your mind." Just the thought brought a smile to her face. Yes, the opportunity to get in the face of the head of James Enterprises was just enough to put her good mood back in place.

Cranking up the radio, she belted out *All I Want for Christmas* right along with Mariah Carey.

"How the heck long is this driveway?" Hope muttered almost two-and-a-half hours later. She'd made the turn where her GPS directed and she was driving up a winding driveway that seemed to lead deeper and deeper into the woods. Snow was falling at a steady rate now and although she had steadily continued to call Ted in hopes of avoiding this detour, his phone was still off.

At the half-mile mark, she spotted a clearing and finally the lodge came into view. "Wow," she gasped at the sight of it. It wasn't overly large. Considering what Diane had said on the phone, Hope was expecting something much bigger. It was magnificent to look at but Hope considered it to be more of a big, private residence than a lodge. The natural wood siding and the green shingled roof looked perfectly in place in this setting–especially with the snow falling. The evergreens surrounding it were all dusted with snow and for a brief moment, Hope almost felt like she was staring at a postcard rather than an actual structure.

Parked over to the right was a huge black SUV so she gave a little sigh of relief that obviously someone was here. She just hoped it was her brother. Parking beside it, she shut off the car and climbed out and stretched. While she loved road trips, she did not love the feeling of being cramped in the car for so long. Purse and phone in hand, she walked up the dozen wooden steps that led to the massive wraparound porch.

At the top of the stairs she stopped and turned around to look at her surroundings. "Beautiful." There was no other word to describe it and yet the word almost seemed too small for what she was seeing. Off in the distance she could see the ski runs and the tracks for the lifts to take skiers to the top. She had to wonder if all of this really went unused now – which would just be a shame.

Turning back toward the door, she took a step forward and almost screamed when Ted appeared. "Hope? What are you doing here?" his voice held both a hint of annoyance and concern. "How did you even find this place?"

Okay, clearly there was still a little hostility left over from Saturday night. Good to know. "I've been trying to call you for hours! Why is your phone off?"

"What?" Ted reached into his pocket and pulled out his phone and turned it on. "Oh. We were working in the car and Mr. James didn't want to be interrupted."

Jerk. It was the immediate thing that came to mind but she kept it to herself. For now. "Well if you'd look at your phone, you'd see you missed about a dozen calls from me and probably at least that many from Merry! It was pretty damn selfish and irresponsible of you to just take off without telling anyone where exactly you'd be and turning off your phone!"

"Yeah, yeah, yeah. Got it. I'm the bad guy," he said sarcastically. "You can't be here, Hope. You have to leave. I'm working. This project is…"

"Yeah, yeah, yeah," she mocked. "Whatever. I wouldn't be here if you would have answered your phone!"

"Get to the point!" he yelled and for a minute, they were both stunned silent.

Hope took a moment to compose herself. She didn't like this side of her brother. He was normally fairly even-tempered and easy to get along with. Just another reason not to like his boss; he was turning Ted into a royal pain in the butt. Taking a deep breath, she decided to just tell him what she had to say. "Merry was in an accident. She…"

"What?" he cried. "When? How? Why didn't she…?"

"Call you?" she interrupted. "Um…yeah. She did. Several times. Just like me."

"Is she all right?"

"I honestly don't know. She tried calling you and…"

"I got it!" he snapped again. "I screwed up! Where is she? How is she?"

"Last I talked to her, the paramedics had just arrived. She was frantic for you, Ted. You need to call her. Now."

Ted immediately took a step away and made the call. Hope wasn't sure what she was supposed to do with herself in the meantime. She was anxious to hear about Merry's condition but she didn't want to hover and eavesdrop either. Moving away to give him privacy, she walked along the front section of the massive porch and took in the scenery. The snow was starting to pick up, as was the wind, and Hope shivered. Snow hadn't seem like a possibility so she wasn't particularly dressed for it. Sure she had on a warm wool coat, but she hadn't thought to pack a hat or gloves.

Or boots.

Looking down at her feet, she frowned at her Uggs. Sure, technically they were boots but not in the practical sense. It was all about the comfort and the look. They weren't going to be any kind of help if she had to walk around in a couple of inches of snow. Shaking her head, she pushed that thought aside. She'd be on her way shortly and hopefully out of the range of this storm.

Not that Knoxville wasn't prone to winter weather. Tara had mentioned how it was going to be cold overnight but during the day they could see temperatures near fifty degrees. Another gust of wind wrapped around her and Hope found she was actually longing for those fifty degrees right now.

Behind her, Ted was busy talking and she couldn't make out much of what he was saying. He was pacing and Hope could only pray Merry was reassuring him that she was fine and only had minor injuries and was already on her way home. It would be the ideal situation and then everyone could move on with their lives.

Two minutes later, she heard Ted curse–another first–and Hope couldn't help but smirk. She pulled herself together before facing him. "Well? How is she?"

He was still pacing. "They're admitting her to the hospital," he said grimly.

"Are you serious? What happened?"

"A guy ran a red light and pretty much totaled her car. Her leg is broken, her arm is broken…" his voice trailed off.

Unable to help herself, Hope walked over and hugged him. "I'm so sorry, Teddy. What do we need to do?"

"Her parents are on their way up from Florida. She called them and they're flying up tonight."

"Well that's a good thing, right?" she asked.

He nodded and then seemed lost in his own thoughts for a moment. "Wait," he said, "how did you get here so fast? Were you following me?"

She rolled her eyes. "Please. Get over yourself. I decided to go to Knoxville to see Tara. We were on the phone the other night and I told her how I had no plans for Christmas so she invited me to join her and her family. I was on the road when I got Merry's call."

"But…how did you know where I was? How did you find this place?"

She knew she couldn't throw Diane under the bus, so she lied. "I pulled over and did a little online research. I've learned enough about your boss over the years so it wasn't too hard to find."

Liar, liar, liar!

"Oh, well…thank you for coming and telling me." He looked nervously over his shoulder. "I need to get back inside."

"Wait. What? You're not serious right now, are you? You need to leave, Ted! You need to go and be with your fiancée! She's hurt and she's scared and she needs you!"

"Her parents are going to be there soon. She'll be fine."

Hope threw up her hands in disgust. "You know what? You're impossible. And you know what else? Right now, I have *zero* respect for you! What kind of man leaves the woman he loves alone when she's hurt? You know what kind? The crappy kind!" She was pacing and her voice was getting louder and louder with each word.

"Hope, you need to…"

"No," she cut him off. "*You* need to man up here, Ted! You need to go in there and tell your boss you have an emergency and you have to go."

"I drove here with him!"

"So? I'll drive you back to Raleigh. End of story!"

He shook his head. "You're going to Knoxville. You have plans."

For a minute, Hope thought her eyes were going to pop out of her head. "Seriously? What is wrong with you?"

"Now what?" he demanded.

"Do you honestly think I would just leave and go on my way and off to Knoxville when you need a ride home? I'll call Tara and explain to her what's going on. She'll completely understand. Getting you back to Merry is the only thing that matters right now."

He still looked uncertain. "It's not that easy, Hope."

She growled with frustration. "That's it," she said and walked toward the front door of the lodge.

"Wait…what are you doing?" Ted called after her. "Hope! Don't go in there! You can't…"

"Mr. James?" she called out as she stepped inside. "Mr. G.B. James? Where are you? We need to talk!"

Ted stormed in behind her and spun her around. "Have you completely lost your mind? You can't just walk into somebody's home and start screaming," he hissed. "I cannot believe you!"

"Oh, yeah? Well I can't believe you either," she hissed right back. "If you're telling me that your job is more important than your fiancée, we're done. You're my brother and I love you but if that's your choice then I have no respect for you."

He stood there and stared at her, his brown eyes wide. "Hope…"

"No, I'm serious, Ted. I can't sit back and watch you work yourself to death. Life is too short," she said and then emotion clogged her throat. "Did you learn nothing from losing mom and dad? They were still young…they had plans for what they wanted to do with their retirement. All the years dad worked so hard and he kept promising mom how once he retired, they'd travel. Once he didn't have to punch a time card, he was going to build that gazebo in the yard she always wanted. Well you know what? That day never came. They were gone before they ever had the chance to do all the things they dreamed of. Is that what you want? To miss out on life because…because of a job?"

"Geez, Hope," he said with a ragged sigh and ran a shaky hand through his hair. "I never," he swallowed roughly, "I never thought of it like that. I thought I was doing the right thing. I need this job and…"

"I get it. I know you need your job but not like this. Not when it means you have to sacrifice so damn much! Now come on. Go and tell Mr. James what happened and let's go."

"I…I just…I don't..."

She was ready to throttle him. "Ted!" she snapped. "Please. Get your stuff and let's go. The snow is coming down heavier and we have a long drive home." Looking around the entryway, which was large with vaulted ceilings, she put her keys down on a table and pulled out her phone. "I'm going to go and call Tara to let her know what's going on. Come on. You need to do this."

Turning her back on him, she walked toward a small sitting area by a fireplace and pulled up her friend's number. Hopefully, her brother was on his way to being the man she thought him to be and telling his boss where he could shove his job and his ridiculous demands. When Tara answered, Hope gave her the Reader's Digest version of what was going on.

"Of course I understand," Tara said. "Go and smack some sense into your brother's head and get him back to Raleigh. I can't believe he was even considering not going."

"I know, I know. How it is that he has a fiancée and I don't is still a mystery," Hope joked.

"You're telling me," Tara laughed. "Go and have a merry Christmas, Hope. We'll have to try this again soon. I've missed you."

"I know. I miss you too. Thanks for being willing to take me in for the holidays."

"It would've been my pleasure. Now go and drive safe, okay?"

"You got it." They hung up and Hope turned around and walked back into the entryway. It was a shame she didn't have more time because just from these two rooms she had seen, the lodge was spectacular. It wasn't swanky in the traditional sense, but it certainly was a classy kind of rustic that was incredibly appealing. "Oh well," she sighed and began to listen for the sound of Ted's footsteps coming her way.

Nothing.

She walked over to the window beside the front door and looked out. "Crap," she muttered. It was still snowing and the footprints she had made just minutes ago outside were already disappearing. "That's not a good sign. Come on, Ted."

Behind her, she finally heard footsteps. Turning around she gasped. "Beckett? What are you doing here?"

Chapter Four

For some reason, it didn't seem odd for Beckett to be standing there. Hope looked at him and smiled. "Did you get called to give up your Christmas too?" And before he could answer, another thought hit her. "Oh, so you've met my brother! Now you know who Ted is!"

"Hope," Beckett began cautiously. "What are you doing here?"

"Ted's fiancé was in a car accident this morning. She couldn't reach him on the phone and I was heading to Knoxville and…"

"Knoxville? What were you going to Knoxville for?"

"I took your advice and decided to spend Christmas with a friend," she said brightly. "Anyway, I was on the road when Merry called and…"

"Merry?"

"Ted's fiancée."

"Seriously? Her name is Merry?"

"I know, right? And it's Christmas!" she giggled. "Anyway, Merry calls and tells me about the accident and the paramedics were just getting there and…"

"She called you from the car? While she was waiting for the paramedics?" he asked incredulously.

She was getting slightly annoyed with his constant interruptions. "As I was saying, she called me when she couldn't reach Ted, so I decided to track him down and let him know in person."

"Where is he?"

"Getting his stuff. He has to get back to Raleigh and be with her. She's pretty banged up."

"He's here to work, Hope," Beckett said with annoyance.

That got her hackles up. "Excuse me?"

"Doesn't she have family or other people who can help her?"

"What difference does that make? She wants Ted. He's her fiancé and she wants him there with her."

"He made a commitment here," Beckett reminded her.

"What's it to you?" she asked, no longer amused or happy with him.

"Oh, Mr. James…there you are," Ted said as he walked down the stairs. "I see you've met my sister."

Everything inside of Hope went cold. *Mr. James?* Beckett was Mr. James? Mr. G.B. James?

And then it hit her…the "B" was for Beckett. Her brain scrambled to try to remember if he had given her any clues as to who he really was. *"I'm a bit of a workaholic and tend to put in the time without being asked."* Well that wasn't a flag raiser. Not really. *"I'm usually too busy in my own office to pay attention to the revolving door of employees." That* seemed to fit the bill a little bit more but not in a way where it would have revealed who he really was.

Beside her, Ted and Beckett were talking in hushed tones, not that she cared. Her mind was still reeling. She needed to grab Ted and get out of here. Soon. Now.

"You can't leave," Beckett said loudly, effectively snapping Hope out of her own thoughts.

"But…my fiancée, she's…she's hurt. I need to go and make sure she's all right."

"Did you speak to her? Did she say she was all right?"

Ted took a small step back. "Sort of. I would just feel better if I could go and check on her myself, sir. Please."

"This is unacceptable, Theodore. You made this commitment to this project and we have a schedule to keep. By you running out of here to go and play nurse is going to put us seriously behind."

"I'll come back tomorrow. I swear. Merry's parents are flying in from Florida tonight. I just hate to think of her being in the hospital all by herself," he said nervously. "Please. You know I never ask for time off."

Beckett studied him hard. "I know you don't

but this is one time when I simply cannot allow it. We have too much to do and by the time you drive all the way back to Raleigh, her parents will already be there and your presence will be pointless."

That was it. Hope had had enough. "Do you even hear yourself?" she demanded as she stepped closer to the two men. "Ted is your employee, not your prisoner. You don't own him. No one planned this. It was an accident for crying out loud. Cut him some slack!"

"Hope," Ted warned. "Please stay out of this."

"No!" she snapped. "I can't stand here and listen to him try to control you! Let's just go. My car is right outside. We can get on the road and you'll be there before you know it."

"If you leave, Theodore, consider your position with James Enterprises terminated," Beckett said sternly.

"What?" Ted croaked. "You can't be serious."

Beckett merely shrugged. "If you can't do your job, then you'll be replaced."

"But I can do my job!" Ted cried out with frustration. "I just need a day to go and check on Merry! Please be reasonable!"

"I am being reasonable. I came here with a very exact schedule that needs to be kept. You assured me you were the person who could handle the work. So I took your word for it and now we're not even here for an hour and you're trying to leave. It seems to me you're the one not being reasonable."

"I'll be back here tomorrow afternoon. I promise. Just…just let me do this and I'll work twice as hard to get us done ahead of schedule."

Hope could only stand there and stare. She couldn't believe what she was hearing. It seemed completely ridiculous and unreasonable and yet…there it was. Her brother was begging for his crappy job, and Beckett? She sighed. And Beckett was a complete tool. That was the real shame in all of this. The man she thought she knew completely didn't exist.

"I need another person here, Theodore," Beckett said tiredly. "There is far too much to do and it required no distractions. If you leave, it's going to put me behind. And you know how I hate when that happens. Deals are lost that way."

Hope was just about to tell Beckett he could take his job and shove it when Ted called out. "Hope can stay with you!"

Both Hope and Beckett stared at him and yelled, *"What?"* at the same time.

Ted's eyes were wild as he took another step back. "I'm serious. Hope can stay here tonight and help you get things started and I'll take her car and go back to Raleigh. You know I'll come back because I wouldn't leave my sister stranded here and…and you'll have someone to assist you. It's a win-win for everyone."

"Ted, have you lost your mind?" Hope yelled. "I just freaked out on him for acting like he owns you and you go and offer me up as a sacrifice as if you have the right to? What is wrong with you?"

"Hope, I need to get home and check on Merry! You said so yourself!"

"Yeah, I get that," she snapped. "But forcing

me to stay here isn't going to help anything. I have no idea what you do except that it has to do with numbers and finance and that's totally not me! And besides, there is no way I'm going to stay here with...*him!*"

Everyone grew silent. Hope refused to look at Beckett but she could feel his eyes on her. Too bad. Whatever relationship she thought they had was over. It didn't matter how great of a kisser he was or how handsome and sexy he was. Dammit. All that mattered was how he was a complete jerk and she just wanted to be away from him.

"Okay," Ted said calmly. "Fine. I won't go. That was wrong of me to expect you to do my job for me. I'm sorry," he said as he looked at Hope.

"It's okay. I know you were just desperate. It's completely understandable."

"If you'll just give me a minute, I'm going to call Merry back and let her know I won't be there. I'll just step out on the porch for some privacy. Please don't leave until I have a chance to say a proper goodbye to you." He walked out the front door, leaving Hope and Beckett alone.

Awkward.

Unable to help herself, she muttered, "I can't believe you couldn't give him twenty-four measly hours to go and check on his fiancée. Like it would've killed you." Walking away from him, she went to stand by the window and watched the snow fall.

Beckett was beside her in an instant. "I value people who honor their word," he said tightly. "I understand his fiancée was hurt, but his presence there wasn't going to change that. She's in the hospital where she has constant care and her family is on its way to her. All your brother was going to do was stand there and be in the way."

Turning her back on the window, she glared at him. "So? Maybe being in the way was what he wanted! What she wanted! Who are you to tell people what they should and shouldn't do? They love each other and that's what you do when you love someone! You're there for one another even if there's nothing you can do to help. Maybe you'd know that if you were actually nice to somebody and they'd want to be with you."

One dark brow arched at her. "Really?" he asked sarcastically.

Hope nodded. "Yes."

"And tell me, does this apply only to those madly in love or would you say it goes for family members too?"

"Of course. Love is love. When you love someone, you want to be there to support them."

"Interesting."

There was something in his tone that didn't sit right. Clearly he was trying to make a point, but she wasn't getting it. "What? What are you saying?"

He shrugged. "Nothing. It just occurred to me that for all you do for your brother, and all the love you show to him, it's not really reciprocated."

"What are you talking about?" she asked wearily, just wanting to be done with him and free to leave.

Without a word, Beckett nodded toward the

window. Hope turned around and gasped. Her brother had stolen her car! All she could see were the taillights disappearing into the forest she had driven through to get here. "No!" she cried and pulled the front door open.

Running down the steps and nearly killing herself slipping and sliding on the slick surface, she hit the ground running and called out after him. "Ted! Ted, come back!!" Obviously, he didn't hear her and soon the car was completely out of sight. And if that wasn't bad enough, Hope looked toward the driveway and saw her luggage and all of her personal belongings in a pile on the ground. "Son of a *bitch!*" she hissed.

She stood frozen in place in total shock by what she had just witnessed. Beckett came up behind her and let out a low whistle. She turned and glared at him over her shoulder.

"That's what love gets you," he said with a cocky grin before he walked over to the driveway and retrieved her things.

"What are you doing?" she asked.

"Like it or not, you're stuck here. At least for tonight. I didn't think you wanted your things to stay out in the snow."

She didn't but she also wasn't ready to concede defeat either. "Are there any hotels nearby? I can call a cab." Beckett didn't appear to be listening as he continued up the front steps and into the house. Dejectedly, she walked up the stairs behind him. She found him in the foyer. "Seriously, I can't stay here."

"Why not?"

"Why not? Isn't that obvious?
You're...you're..."

"I know who I am, Hope."

"Really? Are you sure? Because you seemed
to conveniently leave that out whenever we spent
time together. You knew how much I hated you
and yet..."

He chuckled. "Which is exactly why I didn't
tell you who I was. Believe it or not, I enjoyed
talking with you and spending time with you." He
stepped in close. "I particularly enjoyed kissing
you."

A hot blush crept up her cheeks. She did *not*
want to be reminded of that right now. "Well...that
doesn't matter. Now that I know who you are and
witnessed first-hand how you treat people, it won't
happen again."

"The treating of people or the kissing?" he
asked with a smirk.

She wanted to kick him in the shin and leave
but she was stuck here, for the time being at least.
"Where is the closest hotel?"

"Right here."

She shook her head. "Not happening. I'm not
staying here."

"Hope, it's snowing, you don't have a car and
it's only for one night. There are ten suites here in
the lodge. Trust me. There's more than enough
room for you."

"I don't give a damn about the space, Beckett,"
she snapped. "I don't want to be here with you!"

He studied her for a minute before taking a step
back. "Make yourself at home. I've got some calls

to make."

She stood there completely enraged as she watched him walk away. Shock, anger, outrage…it was all there. Now she just needed to channel that energy into finding a way out of here and away from the insufferable G.B. James.

❧❧❧

Hope stood there for a solid minute in stunned silence. Off in the distance she heard a door close and realized she had thoroughly been dismissed.

"There is no way I'm staying here," she mumbled and pulled her phone out of her bag. The first call she made was to her brother to demand he come back and get her, but–surprise, surprise–he didn't answer. "He's dead when I get my hands on him."

Her only other option to get herself out of Beckett's house was to do a quick Google search for hotels in the area and find a room for the night. It totally sucked and it wasn't quite in her budget, but desperate times called for desperate measures.

Ten minutes later, she had secured a room at a small hotel ten miles up the road. Another Google search helped her to locate a cab service and after giving them her location, the dispatcher didn't seem too confident that they would be able to get a car to her any time soon.

"I'm kind of desperate," she pleaded with him. "My car was stolen and I need to get to a hotel for the night."

"Ma'am," the dispatcher said sympathetically,

"with the way the snow is coming down, even if I had a car available, it would still take about an hour to get to you."

"Please," she said miserably. "I'll even be waiting up by the road. I need to get out of here and to my hotel."

The dispatcher paused for a long moment. "I'll see what I can do, miss. But if I were you, I'd count on it being a minimum of an hour."

It was only a small glimmer of hope but it was something. "Thank you! Thank you so much!" Hanging up the phone, Hope slipped it back into her purse and looked at her belongings. There was her rather bulky suitcase–which, thankfully, was on wheels–and another cooler bag filled with baked goods she had planned on sharing with Tara's family. And her purse.

After several minutes of contemplation, she came to the realization that there was no way she could maneuver it all down the long and winding driveway in the snow. Reaching into the cooler bag, she played around with the tins until she managed to make one with a variety of her favorites in it and then put the rest back. Beckett could have them all if it meant she was getting out of here.

Looking out the window, Hope began to doubt her plan. The snow really was piling up and what if she made it all the way to the end of the driveway and the cab didn't come for hours? Or not at all? Then she'd have to face the humiliation of dragging herself all the way back here and having to beg Beckett for a place to stay.

"Worst. Christmas. Ever." Putting the cooler

bag off to the side, Hope bundled up as best as she could, taking an extra sweater out of her suitcase and putting it on under her coat, and walked out the door.

❧

Beckett paced in his spacious office and called himself every name in the book. What the hell had he been thinking? He knew who Hope was and how she felt about him and at the time it seemed harmless to sort of play with his name and not tell her who he was. But then he'd spent a little more time with her and really connected with her. It was quite the blow to his ego when he realized just how much she hated him. Normally other people's opinions of him didn't matter but with Hope? It did.

And then there was Ted. For a moment it had been almost comical to watch him take off in Hope's car. The look on her face was priceless. But the reality was that Ted had intentionally thrown his sister under the bus and taken the coward's way out. True, Beckett realized, he could have been a little more lenient and let the man go and check up on his injured fiancée, but the reality was what it was–Ted was going to be of no use to his fiancée or anyone. It wasn't the popular opinion, but it was the practical one.

Why couldn't everyone be as practical and see logic like he could? Beckett wondered.

Now his work schedule was shot to hell and he was stuck here with a woman who hated his guts.

He was used to dealing with people's dislike of him, but he hated anyone messing with his work schedule.

James Enterprises ran like a well-oiled machine. Why? Because Beckett made sure it did. He only hired the best and he expected nothing less than one hundred percent dedication from his employees. He didn't grant favors or show favoritism and although it may not win him any awards amongst his employees, they all benefited from the profits he made year after year.

With Ted going off and leaving him, Beckett now faced the task of running numbers solo.

He hated math.

That was what he paid Ted and his entire department for. With a weary sigh, Beckett pulled out the first file he had planned on going over with Ted and scanned through it. His mind was blank. This new project was for a proposed ski resort right here in North Carolina. There were several resorts here already; hell, he was living in one right now, but this new one was going to be better than all of them. Posher. More luxurious. In the simplest terms, it was going to be the ultimate getaway for couples. It would make the Four Seasons look like a Holiday Inn, with guests' every whim being catered to in suites so deluxe they might never want to go outside to ski. In his mind, Beckett saw it all– the rooms, the lobby, all of the amenities.

This extended time away from the office was meant to crunch all the numbers. He already owned the land he was going to use but that was just one tiny aspect of the entire project. The land would have to be cleared, there were construction estimates to consider, trails to set, lifts to install and then came the more intricate details of the resort itself. Decorating, staffing, marketing and advertising…it was endless.

And his numbers man had sneaked off.

Dammit.

Whatever Ted was thinking, he was wrong. There would be no coming back from this. Beckett didn't mess around. Ted's position with James Enterprises was officially terminated. Even if he had left his sister here as some sort of…collateral, it did little to help the situation.

Hope wasn't one of his employees, and she certainly wasn't an accountant. She was a distraction. Even right now, as angry and frustrated as he was and anxious to get to work, all Beckett could think about was where she was and what she was doing. If he was being honest, he hadn't wanted to leave her all alone downstairs. It was simply a way of making sure he kept himself in control. Knowing she was upset over finding out who he really was and then having her brother take off with her car, Beckett had wanted to comfort her and, oddly enough, beg for her forgiveness.

And that was something he'd never done.

Ever.

Beckett had learned a long time ago if you show any weakness, people will take advantage of it. Maybe after today Hope would see it too. She had come here with the simple plan to help her brother out and what had he done? He stole her car and left her with the one man he knew she hated.

How could he possibly turn this situation around? He wanted Hope to be a little less…hostile toward him. That would last all of three seconds if she realized he was going to follow through on his threat to fire her brother. Maybe he should just help her leave and take her to a hotel himself.

That thought stuck with him and Beckett couldn't help but mull it over. Maybe it would be for the best. That way he'd show Hope he respected her feelings about him, even if he didn't like it, and remove all temptation from having her close. Even if it was just for one night, Beckett knew it would be too much. He had far too much work to do and as long as Hope was in the house, he wasn't going to get any of it done.

Raking a hand through his hair, he cursed and moved toward the door. He was known for his control, in every aspect of his life, and somehow the Cooper siblings had managed to royally screw up his day and quite possibly the next several weeks of his life. Another curse escaped as he jogged down the winding stairs to the entryway.

The hairs on the back of his neck tingled and Beckett immediately knew something was wrong. Hope's suitcase was gone and there wasn't a sound in the house. True, there were ten bedrooms and there was the possibility she had chosen one and decided to hunker down and hide out, but he had a feeling that wasn't it.

A quick glance around the entryway and the surrounding rooms, Beckett found no sign of her and turned to look out the front window. Furious with himself and the situation, he saw the footprints in the snow along with what would be tracks from her suitcase being dragged behind her. "Stubborn woman," he growled and pulled his coat from the closet and dug out a pair of snow boots.

He had no way of knowing how long Hope had been gone, but the footprints still looked fresh so hopefully she wasn't far. Stepping out onto the front porch, he knew he had two options: car or snowmobile. The car was readily accessible but with the snow and the unpaved driveway, it could be treacherous. Making his way down the stairs and around to the equipment shed, he opted for the snowmobile. It would take a few extra minutes to get out, but he'd feel safer getting to Hope and getting her back to the house safely.

The entire time he worked, he muttered about unfaithful employees and how if he had his way, he'd make sure Ted Cooper never worked again. Not that it would help anything right now, but it sure made Beckett feel better.

Ten minutes later, he sat astride the Yamaha Venture and made his way slowly out of the shed and into the snow. It was still falling at a steady rate and Beckett couldn't help but feel responsible for Hope wandering around out here all by herself. Granted, she didn't have to leave. That was her own decision, but if she didn't despise him quite so much, she would be sitting safely in the house in front of a fire.

With him.

No time for this! He chided himself and made his way down the winding driveway following her trail of prints. The sky was getting darker, his visibility wasn't great and Beckett was starting to panic that he hadn't come upon her yet. How far could she have walked?

He kept an eye on the prints when they suddenly stopped. He came to a halt and looked around and noticed they didn't just stop, they had slid off to the side and down into the drop off that went down about a dozen feet and led deeper into the forest. Scrambling off the snowmobile, he called out to her. "Hope! Hope, where are you?"

Silence.

Stepping closer to the edge, he looked down and saw her. She was moving around and if his ears weren't deceiving him, she was cursing like a sailor. A chuckle escaped before he could stop it. "Are you all right?" he called down to her.

"Does it look like I'm all right?" she yelled back.

Beckett James was many things, but a rescue-ranger sort, he was not. He was more of a computer geek than an athlete, but seeing Hope slipping around had him stepping up to the challenge. "Okay, okay, I get it. Let me go back up to the house and get some rope so I can pull you up! I'll be back as fast as I can!" As he turned away he was able to make out a few choice words she was using to refer to him but he chose to ignore them and get back to the supply shed. As soon as he turned the snowmobile around, Beckett knew it had been the right choice. The truck would have hampered him in these conditions and he needed to act quickly and get Hope back to the house and out of this cold.

Along with being a computer geek, he was also

super organized. Borderline OCD. When he arrived back at the shed, he knew exactly where to get the rope he needed and also an extra pair of gloves and a hat since he noticed Hope was wearing neither. Five minutes later he had everything he needed and carefully drove back to her.

"I'm going to toss this end of the rope down to you along with a bag that has a hat and gloves to help you out. I want you to tie the end of the rope around your luggage handle and then I'm going to wrap my end around…"

"I get it, Beckett!" she called up to him. "Stop explaining it and toss me the rope! I'm freezing!"

He had a sudden urge to argue back but knew now wasn't the time. Getting Hope up out of the snow was his number one priority. He tossed the rope down and watched as she frantically tied it around her middle and then around the luggage before pulling on the hat and gloves. "Are you ready?"

"Yes!"

That made one of them, Beckett thought. He had wrapped his end around the nearest tree to help; he wasn't sure why he did it, but he knew that's what people did in these situations. Once he got his footing, he began to pull. "I need you to try to walk up the hill, Hope!" he called out. "I know it's slick, but I need you to work with me!"

"I'm trying!"

Snow was falling harder now and Beckett was having a hard time on his end. Between Hope and her luggage and the weather, this wasn't an easy task.

"Beckett!" she called out.

"What? Are you okay?" There was no way for him to see her without letting go of the rope and losing any ground they may have gained.

"I can't do it!" she cried. "My boots...they're not really boots. They've got no traction and my hands and feet are numb. I...I can't make it."

Her voice was getting weaker the longer she spoke and fear began to set in. Beckett was a pro at on-the-spot thinking and one look over his shoulder had the answer. "I'm going to hook up my end to the snowmobile and I think that will help to pull you up without you having to put in too much of an effort. Is that okay with you?"

No answer.

"Hope!" he called out again and when she still didn't answer, his grip loosened on the rope as he tried to step forward and ripped his glove open as well as the palm of his hand. He cursed and quickly went into action. "Stay with me! I'm securing the rope to the snowmobile. Just give me one more minute and I'll have you up here, okay? Hope!"

No answer.

He started the engine and began to move forward slowly while looking over to where Hope would be appearing. It didn't take long for him to spot the blue knit hat peering out over the snow. He called her name and kept talking to her until he got her all the way up on level ground and then cut the engine and ran over to her, dropping to his knees when he reached her side.

"Hope? Hope, come on, sweetheart. Open your eyes. Talk to me," he coaxed as he quickly got the rope off of her and her suitcase. His hand was bleeding and he was starting to get numb from the cold but he needed her to wake up so he could get her on the snowmobile and get them back to the house. He felt for her pulse and almost cried with relief when he found it. Patting her cheek, he gently called her name again.

Long eyelashes fluttered open as she seemed to blink him into focus. "Beckett?" she whispered. "What…? How…?"

"Come on," he said. "You're soaked to the skin and we need to get you warmed up. Can you stand for me?"

"No, I can't stand you," she muttered as she gingerly came to her feet.

Beckett couldn't help but laugh. The snarky comeback meant she was going to be all right. He helped her climb onto the back of the vehicle and then secured her luggage. His mind was racing with a million questions about why she thought walking around in a blizzard was a good idea, but he held his tongue.

Climbing on, he turned and looked over his shoulder. "You need to wrap your arms around me and hold on. I can't go too fast but you need to hold on to me. Okay?"

Hope nodded slowly, her eyes drifting closed.

"Hope! I need you to stay awake." Reaching behind him, he pulled her arms around him and secured her hands against his middle. With one hand, he started the snowmobile up, carefully turned them around and slowly made their way up the winding drive. Five minutes later, they pulled up to the front steps of the house. He'd put the snowmobile away later. Right now the only thing that mattered was getting Hope warmed up. A little shaky on his feet, Beckett scooped her up into his arms and carefully climbed the stairs to the porch and opened the front door.

"Norma!" he called out. "Norma, we need a hand!"

"Norma?" Hope mumbled. "Who the heck is Norma?"

"The housekeeper," he replied and gave a tight smile when an elderly woman entered the entryway from the kitchen.

"Oh, my goodness!" she cried. "What happened? I didn't know you had gone out!"

Beckett gave a quick rundown of the situation. "Miss Cooper is going to need a hot bath drawn immediately. Put her in one of the suites on the second floor and she's going to need some dry clothes. All of hers are still in her suitcase outside and are most likely frozen."

"Maybe they're not," Hope said as she wiggled to get out of his arms.

"We'll be inside by the fire," Beckett said to the housekeeper. "Please go get the tub running and we'll be up in a minute."

"Yes, Sir," she said and quickly made her way up the stairs.

"Poor woman," Hope mumbled.

Beckett ignored her and walked over to the study that was off the entryway. There was a fire blazing in there and he sat them down in front of it before peeling the hat and gloves off of her. Next came her boots as she slowly removed her coat.

"Oh! What happened to your hand?"

Beckett looked down and remembered he had sliced it open on the rope. He had been so consumed with worry for Hope that he had completely forgotten about it. "It's nothing. Don't worry about it. We need to get you warm." He yelled out for Norma to see if the bath was ready but the woman didn't respond.

"It's not nothing," Hope said, her voice laced with concern. She pulled his hand into hers and looked at it. "It's pretty deep." She gingerly touched it and winced right along with him. "Norma! Bring a first-aid kit with you, please!"

"Hey!" Beckett snapped, pulling his hand back. "I'm perfectly capable of taking care of this myself. You're the one who needs to be tended to. You probably have hypothermia by now. What the hell were you thinking walking around in the snow like that?"

"Oh, I don't know, maybe that I wanted to get away from you?" Hope pulled back to put some space between them. "I told you I wanted to leave. You could have called me a cab, or better yet, driven me to a hotel, but no. You demanded that I stay here. I'm not one of your employees, Beckett. You can't tell me what to do." She crossed her arms across her chest and prayed Norma would arrive and tell her the bath was ready.

"What are you? Twelve?"

Hope glared at him. "Whatever. And you need to do something about that cut. Don't expect me to play nurse and fix your hand."

Now there was an image that was going to stick in his mind: Hope dressed up as a nurse…a sexy nurse. Hell, he had almost been able to push aside the mental images of her dressed up as Princess Leia in the gold bikini and now he had the nurse one to contend with. Before he could comment on it, Norma walked hurriedly back into the room with a first aid kit in one hand and a towel in the other.

"If you'll come with me, Miss…?"

"Cooper. Hope Cooper," Hope said as she stood up.

"Your bath is ready and I've put a robe in the bathroom for you to put on when you're done until your clothes are warm and dry again."

"Thank you."

The women exited the room and Beckett watched them leave before sitting back in his chair and letting out a ragged breath. The day had gotten completely out of control and he had no idea how to make it right again. Work was out of the question. His hand was throbbing and he needed to make sure the rest of Hope's things got into the house and dried.

Putting the first-aid kit aside, he rose and walked out the front door, gathered the luggage and brought it back inside. Then he turned right back around and drove the snowmobile to the shed and put it away along with the rope. Looking around, Beckett couldn't help but wipe down the snowmobile and make sure the rags he used were put in the laundry bin. Everything looked to be in its place, until he saw how the rope wasn't coiled as tightly as he preferred.

Thirty minutes later, the shed was completely back in order and he walked through the snow back into the house. Norma was walking toward the study with a tray containing a couple of steaming mugs.

"Miss Cooper's clothes are all in the dryer and she just finished her bath. I made you both mugs of hot chocolate. It feels like the perfect day for it." She placed the tray down on a table facing the fireplace. "I was going to put out some of the cookies I baked, but Miss Cooper said she had an entire insulated bag full of them. She told me she'd take some out when she comes down. How is your hand?"

Crap. He had forgotten about it again. Instinctively, he flexed it several times and winced with each movement. Not only that, he felt it bleeding again. "It's fine," he lied. "I'm going to clean it up and get a bandage on it."

"Do you need any help? I've done my fair share of bandaging up all kinds of scrapes and cuts between my kids and grandkids."

It wasn't that Beckett didn't trust Norma; he completely did. He just didn't like anyone fussing over him. He was a grown man and he could handle cleaning his own injuries and putting on a bandage. "Thanks but I think I've got it."

Norma nodded and left the room.

When Beckett was alone, he sat down in one of the chairs and put the towel Norma had brought in earlier across his lap. The cut was on his left hand and right now that was the good news. The cut was deep and probably could have used a couple of stitches, but there was no way he was going to get to an ER in this storm.

Opening the first-aid kit, he fished out the peroxide and antiseptic wipes along with a couple of gauze pads and tape. The cut was too big and in too awkward of a position for a regular bandage so he resigned himself to wrapping the palm of his hand all the way around to keep it clean.

He was just pouring the peroxide onto his hand when Hope walked in. A loud breath hissed out at the stinging sensation. Before Beckett knew it, Hope was in front of him with his injured hand in hers and blowing on the wound. He stared at her, completely stupefied by her gesture. Her hair was damp and curling wildly and she didn't have on a stitch of makeup. She was completely engulfed in one of the spa-style robes he had stocked when this house was used as a ski lodge.

It shouldn't have looked sexy, but it did.

"Are you seriously just cleaning this now?" she asked, effectively snapping him out of his reverie.

"I needed to bring the luggage in and get the snowmobile and rope put away."

"That should have taken all of five minutes, Beckett. I know I was easily upstairs for almost forty-five minutes." She blew on the spot again before gently wiping his hand with the edge of the towel that was in his lap. Without asking, she picked up a pack of the antiseptic wipes and finished cleaning his hand before examining it a little more closely. "You probably need stitches."

"Not gonna happen," he said, his throat feeling a little tight.

Hope looked up at him, her eyes huge. "Why?"

A chuckle escaped before he could stop it. "The snow? The storm? Any of this ringing a bell?"

"Right. Of course," she said as a blush colored her cheeks. "Sorry." Her focus went back to his hand and she found some butterfly bandages to pull it together, then wrapped it in gauze and taped it. "There. That should do for now." Her voice was slightly breathless as she looked back up at him.

In that instant, Beckett knew he could spend an entire lifetime staring into her eyes and never get enough. She was beautiful and when she went to pull her hand away from his, he held on. His name was a mere whisper on her lips and he almost groaned at the sound of it. He wanted her in the worst way but he knew it was too soon. Her feelings for him were too raw and too negative for him to really convince her he wasn't such a bad guy.

Hope cleared her throat. "Um…thank you," she said quietly, her hand still in his. "For coming to get me. I didn't think I was going to be able to get out of there on my own and I had no idea how far I'd gotten from the house or how far I was from the road."

Beckett wanted to remind her how she never should have left, that her rash decision could have cost her her life. That's what he wanted to do. That's what G.B. James would do. But as he continued to look down into her eyes, something inside of him softened. "You're welcome," he said gruffly and was rewarded with a smile.

Chapter *Five*

Hope was the first to look away as she scrambled to her feet. She nervously looked around but was at a loss for what to do with herself.

"Norma made us some hot chocolate," Beckett said and gestured to the tray beside him. "She also mentioned you had some cookies with you. Or was that just a rumor?" His lips quirked as he watched her walk across the room and out into the entryway.

With the large bag in her hand, Hope strode back into the room. "Not a rumor," she said and sat down in the chair beside him, unzipping the bag. "I had brought enough to share with Tara's whole family so we have quite the variety to choose from."

With no other way to do it, Hope pulled out each tin, all eight of them, and then remembered the one that was in her purse. Without a word, she jumped up and found her purse by the front door, carried it back into the study and pulled out the last tin. Beckett's eyes were as wide as his smile as he watched her.

"How many people are in her family?" he joked.

"I have no idea but after the way things went with Ted last week, there was no way I was sharing any more with him. This is everything I prepared."

Beckett eyed the pile of cookie tins and then Hope and then the tins again. "How many cookies would you say you made? Total. Including what you brought to the office over the last couple of weeks."

She chuckled and shook her head. "You don't want to know."

"I do! I'm curious. Come on. Fess up."

Hope sat down and leaned back in her chair and did the mental math. "Okay, I made twelve different kinds of cookies and made about four dozen of each so that's…"

"Over five hundred cookies," Beckett finished for her.

"I really do hate math," she sighed and reached for her mug of hot chocolate. "It makes my brain hurt."

"Mine too."

They sat in companionable silence while Beckett helped himself to the first tin of cookies. "God, Hope, how do you do it?" he asked with a sigh. "I'm not normally someone who goes crazy for sweets but these are like crack."

"Ted says the same thing." As soon as it was out of her mouth, she remembered her anger toward her brother and, in turn, her anger at Beckett.

Primly, she faced the fireplace and sipped on her hot chocolate.

"I'm guessing by the sudden silent treatment, we're back to being adversaries."

"We never stopped," Hope said quietly. "And thanks to you, my brother took off and left me here."

It was pointless to argue. Beckett knew he had pushed, no more than usual, but he had pushed Ted into doing something drastic. He just didn't think he'd take it out on his sister. Although Beckett knew all too well what it felt like to be betrayed by a sibling, he hated seeing Hope suffer the same fate.

"He could have taken you with him," Beckett said after several long minutes of silence.

"I'm not going to discuss this with you. Ted and I rarely argue. Never have. The only thing that seems to put us at odds is his job."

Beckett turned in his seat and faced her. "What is it that you find so offensive about his job? Ted seems to enjoy it and he's really good at what he does."

Hope put her mug down with a little too much force and some of the chocolaty liquid spilled over. "Are you sure you want to know?" she asked and Beckett nodded. "Ted works a ridiculous amount of hours. He has no personal time for himself and for all the time he puts in, he still struggles financially. You don't compensate him for all the work he does because you've put him on a salary rather than an hourly wage. Of course, *that* works in your favor so I'm not really surprised."

"And…?"

"Just because someone works for you doesn't mean you own them. Employees are entitled to their weekends, holidays, and time with their families. You've made it so they have to choose and if they choose their lives, you threaten them with their jobs."

"That's not…"

"That's exactly what you did earlier with Ted. Tell me, is he fired? If he comes back tomorrow as he said he would, are you going to let him walk back in here and go back to work?" She didn't let him answer. "No. You won't. Ted will show up here and apologize and beg for your forgiveness but it won't matter. You'll fire him and you won't even feel bad about it. It will be Jerome all over again."

"Okay, what is it with you and Jerome? Was he your friend?" Beckett asked with impatience.

"No. I had only met him once, but he was incredibly sweet and Ted told me how he was working for you because he needed the insurance because his wife was ill. But you don't take the time to know these things about your employees. They're just numbers on a page to you. You don't take note of who they really are or what's important to them. They're meaningless to you unless they're sitting at a desk and doing work for you."

"That's a little harsh."

"Am I lying?" she asked, her voice dripping with sarcasm.

Seemingly unwilling to answer right away, Beckett took a sip of his beverage and looked into the fire. "You know, Hope, sometimes things aren't always what they seem."

She snorted with disbelief.

"It's true. I used to run my business in a very different way. But you know what happens when you're too nice to people?"

"They actually like you?"

He laughed softly. "No. They take advantage of you. Or steal your car and leave you stranded."

Hope glared at him. "That was a low blow."

"Doesn't make it any less honest," he said with a shrug.

"Say what you want, but the fact still remains that you are a bit of a tyrant where your employees are concerned and I'm surprised you don't have more turnover."

"There's enough turnover," he said blandly, "but I don't see it as a bad thing. To me, that means I'm weeding out the weaker ones and am left with the ones with a strong work ethic."

"Or the ones who are too scared or can't afford to be unemployed."

"Whatever works."

Hope stared at him, wide-eyed. "What could have possibly happened to you in your life to make you this way?"

Without looking at her, Beckett stood and finished his hot chocolate. "I've got some work to do. Dinner is at six." And with that, he left the room.

Hope sat back and slowly finished her own drink while thinking about Beckett. The fact that he had jumped up and left so quickly told her she'd touched on a nerve. Something had indeed happened to make him this way. And if her gut was telling her anything, it had to do with his family, which would completely make sense from all the things he'd shared with her.

Placing her mug down on the tray beside his, she stood and took it to the kitchen in hopes of talking to Norma. Maybe she could unlock some of the mystery as to why Beckett was the way he was.

Sure enough, Norma was in the kitchen washing vegetables. She looked up and smiled when she saw Hope standing in the doorway. "How are you feeling? Warmer, I hope."

"Much," Hope replied and placed the tray on the counter next to the sink. "Thank you for the hot chocolate. It was delicious."

"You are more than welcome." She was silent for a moment while she finished her task, then shut off the water. As Norma reached for a dish towel to dry her hands, she turned toward Hope. "If you don't mind my asking, what were you doing wandering around in the snow like that?"

Awkward. Deciding to go for the brutal truth, Hope took a steadying breath. "Honestly? I was walking to the road in hopes of getting a ride to a hotel. I had called for a cab but they weren't sure if they'd get here. I knew the roads would be more manageable than that winding driveway so I just thought I'd speed up the process and meet them."

Norma tsked at her. "There are plenty of rooms here. Why would you go to another hotel?"

"Because I don't want to be here. I came here to get my brother and after arguing with Beckett, Ted took off with my car and left me here."

"Beckett?" Norma asked, a look of amusement

on her face.

"Oh, I'm sorry. Mr. James." Hope cringed at the thought of this woman being offended by her use of Beckett's first name. Knowing him, he probably expected everyone to be formal with him, even in his own house.

"No, no," Norma chuckled. "I'm just surprised you called him Beckett."

"I'm confused. What am I supposed to call him?"

"His family calls him Gabriel."

"Gabriel?" Hope mimicked and then it hit her, there was the "G" in G.B. James. The man was infuriating. How many other names was he hiding? "When he introduced himself to me several weeks ago, he said his name was Beckett."

"Oh, he's gone by that one too, but those of us who've known him since he was little, know him as Gabriel."

"How long have you known him?"

"Since he was a baby," Norma said with a hint of pride. "I've known the James family for a very long time."

Jackpot! "Why doesn't he talk to his family?"

Norma turned away and began moving the vegetables over to a cutting board. "You know how family can be."

Hope moved until she was standing opposite Norma, facing her. "Yes, I do know how family can be but it seems to me like Beckett has a lot of trust issues because of his family and it's affecting his entire life. Do you think they'll ever reconcile?"

"You care for him," Norma said, placing her

hands on the butcher block, a serene smile on her face.

"*What?!* No…no," Hope said but even she didn't believe her own words and then sighed. "It's…it's complicated. When I met Beckett, I didn't know who he was. What I did know was I hated G.B. James. It wasn't until I got here today that I realized they were one and the same."

"It seems to me if you liked Beckett, it shouldn't matter how he's also G.B. James."

Hope shook her head. "It's not that easy. It's like he is two different people. The man I got to know and went out with was sweet and funny and charming. And then I saw him with my brother and it was like someone had flipped a switch." She shook her head again. "I don't know for sure who he really is but I'm thinking it's the control-freak-office-tyrant."

Norma laughed and began to chop the vegetables. "Miss Cooper…"

"Hope," she corrected.

"Hope…I've known that man his entire life. He has his reasons for being the way he is. That's not to say I agree with it. I think he'd feel a whole lot better if he learned to relax more and work less." She chuckled. "Although if I live to see that day I might think I was hallucinating!"

"Can't you talk to him?" Hope asked. "Can't you convince him to be a little more…flexible? Forgiving?"

"Oh, I've tried. Believe me." Norma stopped her task again and looked around the kitchen. "There was a time when this house was filled during the holidays with the entire family. I used to love to decorate and cook and bake…everything was so festive! Now, though, it's just a sad shell of its former glory. I miss those days. I miss the chaos and the laughter and…the people." She sighed. "Look around this place; Christmas is less than a week away and you'd never know it around here."

"It is kind of depressing," Hope agreed. "So he doesn't even put up a tree?"

Norma shook her head. "Not in almost six years. The first few years after his father died, everyone else still came but it wasn't the same. And then…" She sighed again. "Then everyone stopped coming."

"Do you live here full-time?"

"Pretty much. Although I'm not needed the way I used to be."

"Do you have any family close by you're going to spend Christmas with?"

"I do, but I always feel guilty leaving him here. I invite him to come with me, but he always declines."

"When do you leave?"

"Oh, I only leave for a couple of hours. Even though he says it doesn't bother him to be alone and that Christmas isn't a big deal, I can't stand it for him. Nobody ought to be alone on Christmas."

Hope agreed. "I feel the same way. When Ted told me he had to come here to work, I was devastated. We just lost our parents a couple of months ago and we only have each other. With him working, I was going to be alone. I was heading to

Knoxville to be with a friend when I had to make a detour to come here." She shared the story of Merry's accident. "I didn't expect Ted to act so impulsively and just leave me here. I just hope he comes back tomorrow and maybe I can salvage my own Christmas."

Norma turned and looked out the window. "This storm seemed to come out of nowhere. I was watching the weather report and I don't think it's expected to let up anytime soon. I'd be surprised if your brother actually could get back here."

"Please don't say that," Hope said dejectedly. "I don't think I could stand it if I were stranded here. No offense."

Norma chuckled. "None taken." She studied Hope for a minute. "Just a word of advice to you; don't judge Beckett too harshly. You obviously saw some good in him, which is more than I can say for most people. You may be the one who breaks through the wall he's built around himself."

"I don't think so," Hope said and took a step back. "Maybe if he had been honest with me about who he really was, but he wasn't. He lied to me." She shook her head. "That's a big no-no in my book."

"He's really not all that bad, Hope. Trust me. Spend some time with him. You'll see."

Taking her own turn looking out the window Hope sighed. It wasn't like she had much of a choice. With the way the snow was coming down, she was going to have nothing else to do but spend time with Beckett James.

She only hoped she didn't end up regretting it.

❧

At six o'clock sharp, Beckett sat opposite Hope at his dining room table. It was big enough to seat twenty and now that they were there, he couldn't help but laugh at how ridiculous it looked.

"What?" Hope asked. "What's so funny?"

He gestured to the table. "I guess I should have asked Norma to set us up someplace else. This table is a little, shall we say…large, for just two people."

Hope laughed too. "Whew. I thought it was just me!" She looked down at their plates which were filled with roast beef, red skinned potatoes and grilled asparagus and sighed with appreciation. "Is there someplace else to eat?"

Beckett stood and picked up his and Hope's plates. "Follow me."

She did and was surprised when they were back in the kitchen. Norma's eyes went wide at the sight of them.

"That table is too big for two people," Beckett said and put the plates down on the much smaller farm-style table. "Have you eaten yet, Norma?"

"N…no," she said, seemingly stunned.

"Well, make up a plate and join us," he said and held out a chair for Hope and then went back to the dining room to get their glasses.

Hope watched in amusement as Norma made herself a plate and sat down at the table. "Tell me this isn't the first time he's done this?" she asked.

"Never," Norma whispered. "Even when he's

115

here all by himself, he always eats in the dining room.

Hope wasn't sure what to make of that so she chose to keep quiet. A minute later, Beckett strode back into the kitchen and placed their drinks down. "Norma? What can I get you to drink?"

"Um…"

Without waiting for a response, he walked over to the stove and put on the tea kettle. "What was I thinking? You usually have tea with your meals, right?"

"Um…"

The whole thing was a bit comical to Hope, and confusing. The poor woman was clearly confused by her boss's behavior and it seemed to her that Beckett was either trying really, really hard to change her perception of him or he had hit his head on something. The thought almost made her laugh so she opted to start a conversation. "How's your hand?"

Beckett shrugged and began to cut into his roast beef. "It's a little painful, but I think I'll live," he said with a wink. "Sorry to disappoint you."

She blushed at his comment. "That wasn't what I was thinking. Much."

"You have a very expressive face, Hope. It gives you away every time."

Now that she had that tid-bit of information, she made a mental note to be a little more aware of herself. "Anyway, did you get any work done?" She hated even bringing it up, but she wasn't sure what else to talk about.

"Not really. Most of what I had planned dealt

with the numbers and that's Ted's area of expertise. Mostly I'm looking at the plans and the drawings and seeing what it is I can do on my own."

"Or you could take this as an opportunity to actually rest and not work," Norma said.

Beckett placed his silverware down gently and smiled. "Haven't we had this discussion a hundred times before? And hasn't my answer always been the same?"

"It has and it's about time you mixed it up a bit. You know. Try something different."

"Different," he snorted playfully. "I have too much to do that needs to stay on schedule to try to do something...different."

"Nonsense," Norma said, rising to make her tea. "I'm not saying you have to go out and try bungee jumping or anything, but you have a guest here and maybe she'd like to see the rest of the lodge or the property."

"It's dark out, Norma," he replied. "It's too dangerous to go out and see the property. Besides, I think Hope saw enough of it today."

"That's for sure," Hope chimed in. "But I would not be opposed to a tour of the lodge. From what I've seen so far, it's beautiful. I can't believe you haven't decided to convert this into your new resort. You have plenty of room and the lifts are already here. Why not just rehab this one?"

"It's...it's complicated," he said carefully and Hope could tell he was really trying to not be annoyed by her question.

Rather than argue with him or push him, she merely shrugged. "Okay."

He looked up at her with surprise. "Okay? That's it? You've got nothing else to say to me? No snarky comeback?"

"What would be the point? You have your reasons for doing the things you do. It's your business, not mine." She took a forkful of her dinner and when she finished it, she turned to Norma. "Everything is delicious. Thank you so much."

"It's my pleasure. It's nice having people in the house to cook for. It doesn't happen nearly enough."

Beckett coughed and then looked over at Norma. "Seriously? Still?"

"Can't blame a girl for trying," she said and went back to her meal.

"Anyway," Beckett began, looking over at Hope, "any word from your brother?"

She shook her head. "I've tried to call him several times, but he's not answering. I'm sure he thinks that by avoiding my calls today that I'll be calmer tomorrow. But he's wrong. If anything, I'm getting angrier the longer her ignores me."

"Oh he's not going to get here tomorrow," Norma said and took a sip of her tea.

"What do you mean?" Beckett asked.

"The snow's still coming down pretty heavy and the temperature is supposed to drop way down overnight so the roads are going to freeze. They're already talking about shutting down the interstate. I'd say you'd be lucky if you saw him in two to three days."

"No!" Hope said a little too desperately. "That

can't be right! Beckett? Have you watched the weather? Is that really a possibility?"

He didn't make eye contact with her as he cut another slice of roast beef. "I'm sure it is," he said casually. "It's one of the hazards of living up in the mountains."

"Don't they have plows? If this is a common occurrence, why aren't there preventions to make sure the roads are clear?"

"Sometimes you can only do so much, Hope. You can't control the weather and they'll plow as much as they can but sometimes it's too dangerous for the plows to stay out there." As much as he understood Hope's concerns, Beckett had hoped she had relaxed a little and wasn't quite so anxious to leave.

"I guess," she said quietly.

"How about his fiancée? Merry. Have you tried calling her?" Beckett asked.

"Her cell must be off and I'm not sure what hospital she's in. I called the one she works at but she's not there. After that, I just gave up. I don't want to upset her too."

"Seems to me like you're a lot more considerate of everyone else's feelings than they are of yours," he said carefully.

"I'm aware. I guess there hasn't been anything else to bring it to the surface like what happened today. And last week."

"What happened last week?" Norma asked.

Hope looked shyly over at Beckett.
"We…um…we argued over the length of time Ted was going to be here working. We were having

dinner at the office and he threw me out."

Norma's eyes went wide and Beckett sat back and watched Hope. "From what you told me about the dinner, you were lucky to escape."

Hope laughed. "Ugh…it really was the worst dinner I've ever had. I can't believe it was one of Ted's favorites."

"Maybe that's just what he tells her."

"God I hope so," Hope said. "I know I'm not the greatest cook in the world but I know the meals I make for him are better than that!"

"The chicken pot pie was amazing," Beckett said and then snapped his mouth shut.

"How…how do you know?" Hope asked, confusion written all over her face.

"You left a lot of it for him and later that night when we were working, Ted offered me some." He shrugged and looked back at her. "It was one of the best meals I ever had."

"Hey!" Norma said with a chuckle. "I'm sitting right here!"

"No offense," he said quickly and looked between the two women, unsure of what he was supposed to say to get himself out of the situation. "I mean…um…it was…"

"Oh, knock it off," Norma said and waved it off. "There's nothing wrong with enjoying someone else's cooking. I snuck some of the cookies earlier and if the pot pie was half as good as those were, then you were one hundred percent correct in what you were saying!"

Both Beckett and Hope seemed to sag with relief at the same time. "Well thank you," Hope said. "It's nice to hear that my cooking and baking are appreciated."

"The cookies were the talk of the office," Beckett said.

"I thought you didn't pay attention to what your employees are doing or saying or anything like that," Hope reminded him.

"Well, I pay attention sometimes."

"Sometimes?"

"Especially when I'm standing around a table with a dozen people who are arguing over some sort of peppermint chocolate thing." He smiled. "I got the last one."

"I think I have a few more of them in one of the tins."

"So where were you taking all those baked goodies to, Hope?" Norma asked.

"I was going to spend Christmas with a friend over in Knoxville before I got detoured here. I called her and let her know what was going on, well, at least what was going on at the time. Last I talked to her, I thought I was driving Ted back to Raleigh. She has no idea Ted took off with my car."

"Maybe you'll still get there," Norma said with a hint of hope in her voice.

Hope shook her head. "I doubt it. Even if by some chance Ted did get back here tomorrow, I'd have to take him all the way back to Raleigh and I just don't have it in me to drive all the way back out this way and beyond again. It just wasn't meant to be."

"Why will you have to take him home? Won't

he be coming back to work?"

Hope looked at Norma and then at Beckett. He was busy eating and studying his plate. "Ted won't be working for James Enterprises anymore," she said quietly and went back to her own plate of food.

The remainder of the meal was spent in silence.

Hope was standing by the window in the study watching the snow fall. It didn't seem like it was ever going to stop. Norma was right; there was no way for Ted to get back here tomorrow so that meant she had another full day with Beckett. Not that she had been spending all that much time with him, but still.

If this version of Beckett was the only one she knew, it wouldn't feel like such a bad thing to be stuck here. From what she'd seen of it, the house was beautiful and Beckett had been genuinely nice to her. Unfortunately, she knew the other side of him, the real side, and she couldn't get past it no matter how hard she tried.

Hope sighed as she looked at the night sky. Her mother had always said you shouldn't judge a book by its cover and normally she agreed with that logic. The problem was that for the five years Ted had worked for James Enterprises, she'd heard nothing but negative comments on the way Beckett, or G.B. James, treated his employees. Although, if she really thought about it, Ted never really complained about it. It was her own perception of the things her brother described. Could she possibly be wrong?

She shook her head. No way. She had witnessed first-hand the way Beckett had spoken to Ted about leaving. He was cold, unyielding and condescending. But…she'd also witnessed first-hand how he could be sweet and funny and charming.

Would the real Beckett James please stand up?

Another sigh escaped. Why did this have to be so complicated? Like life wasn't difficult enough right now, why did all of this have to happen? How cruel was it that she finally met a guy, a great guy, and he wasn't the man she'd thought he was. It was like the universe was just wiping its feet on her.

Yeah, merry freaking Christmas to me, she thought.

Stepping away from the window, she stretched and walked over to the fire. It had been a long time since she'd had the opportunity to sit in front of a real wood-burning fire, probably not since she had gone camping as a kid. The fireplace was magnificent; the entire front of it was covered in stone and the mahogany mantle was huge. It was rustic yet regal all at the same time and Hope couldn't help but to pull a chair closer.

If she wasn't so full from dinner, she'd be tempted to ask Norma for another mug of her hot chocolate. Maybe she would do that later. For now, she was content to simply have the room to herself to enjoy the warmth of the fire.

"That's one of my favorite spots," Beckett said as he slowly came into the room. "Especially on a night like this." He took the chair beside her and moved it forward and closer to hers.

"I figured you'd be in your office working," Hope said, purposely looking into the fire and not at him. Just the sight of Beckett was enough to weaken her resolve to dislike him.

"Like I said at dinner, without Ted, there isn't as much for me to do. Besides, I thought you mentioned taking a tour of the place."

Hope shrugged. "It's not a big deal. Judging by the way the snow is still falling, I'll be here all day tomorrow too. So don't feel like you have to entertain me. I'm perfectly content sitting here by the fire."

"You may find this hard to believe, but I'm feeling pretty content right now too."

Now she couldn't help but look at him. "Really?" she asked with disbelief. "You? The workaholic. The man who forces people to leave their families at Christmas so you can work. You're content to just sit here and look at the fire." She rolled her eyes. "Give me a break."

"It's not looking at the fire that has me feeling content, Hope," he said softly. "It's sitting by the fire with you."

She snorted with disbelief. "Please. You've been here all of thirty seconds. Although, maybe that's a long attention span for you. I don't know."

He chuckled beside her and shifted until he was facing her. "Tell me, do you give everyone you dislike this hard of a time or is it just me?"

"I've never disliked anyone to the degree that I dislike you," she said honestly. "For the most part, I get along with everyone."

"Well, if you really think about it, we get along very well. As a matter of fact, I think we get along great. It's the things you *think* you know about me that are tripping you up."

Wasn't that almost exactly what she was telling herself earlier? What was he, some kind of mind reader? Unfortunately, she couldn't seem to form any words to respond to him, which he obviously seemed to know because now he was smirking.

Jerk.

"How about this," he began. "How about we pretend I'm not G.B. James, your brother's boss and…"

"You fired him so technically, you're not his boss anymore."

Beckett frowned. "Then let's just pretend we don't know anything about James Enterprises. We're just two people who met here at a ski lodge and we're getting to know each other. How about that?"

"Beckett…"

"I'm serious," he said, a smile crossing his face. "We'll walk around the lodge and talk and just…get to know one another. Please, Hope. I know we've spent some time talking but there's still so much more I want to know about you."

She eyed him suspiciously and thought about his offer. "If I agree to this, and that's a pretty big if, then I'm going to want to know about you. And you can't get all sulky and pout and clam up. If I ask you something about you or your family, you have to answer. Deal?"

Now it was Beckett's turn to look at her

suspiciously. "Deal."

"Wow, you didn't even take too long to think about it. I'm impressed."

"Believe it or not, Hope, I'm not the ogre you think I am."

"Your actions earlier today say otherwise."

He sighed with frustration. "The whole situation took me by surprise. I don't like surprises. I came up here with a very specific agenda and I didn't think anything could interfere with that. Obviously I was wrong."

"Obviously."

He quirked a brow at her. "Okay, if we're going to play the getting-to-know-you game, you have to be a little less snarky."

"Fine."

Both brows rose at that one. "Really? No argument?"

She shook her head. "You're right. I'm being sarcastic and snarky and closing my mind to everything and that's not who I really am. Like I said earlier, I really do tend to get along with everyone. This year, this season in particular, is just hard for me and for some reason, you're the guy who I'm taking it out on."

"I've been an easy target," he said with a slight laugh.

She nodded. "Really, I should be thanking you then. If I didn't have a way of letting out all of this anger and aggression, I'd probably go crazy and just explode."

"We can't have that," he teased. "And for what it's worth, I'm happy to be your…punching bag or target or whatever it is you want to call it. If it helps you, then I don't mind."

"You're being far too kind, Beckett," Hope said shyly. "I can't believe we're even having this discussion. For all the years Ted worked for you, we never met. I had this image in my mind of who G.B. James was, and I have to tell you, it wasn't you."

"Is that a good thing or a bad thing?"

She studied his face for a long time. "I'm not sure yet."

He nodded slowly. "I can handle that." He stood and held out a hand to her. "Come on. Let's go and take a look around. We'll go through the house and then outside for a bit on the back deck. The lighting back there is breathtaking in the snow, like a winter wonderland."

Hope couldn't believe it, but she readily reached out and put her hand in his. "Then I guess this place is aptly named."

Beckett carefully pulled her to her feet. "What do you mean?"

"I saw some of the signs as I was walking down the driveway earlier. This place used to be called Winter Park. If the view is how you described, I'm just saying the name fits."

Beckett didn't respond, but he did pull her in close. "You scared the hell out of me earlier, you know that right?" His arms slowly slid around her waist.

Hope's breath caught in her throat. "I didn't mean to scare you," she said softly, looking up into his dark eyes.

"I know. You meant to piss me off," he chuckled softly as one hand came up to caress her cheek. "I'm glad I found you."

"Me too. I can't even begin to think what would have happened if you hadn't come when you did."

"That's not what I meant," he said quietly, and bent his head toward hers.

"Beckett…"

And then his lips touched hers and silenced her. Hope was too surprised to react at first. It was everything she remembered–soft, exciting and very arousing. The man certainly knew how to kiss. As if they had a mind of their own, her arms came up and rested on Beckett's broad shoulders. They were pressed together from head to toe.

His lips were slowly sipping from hers as if he were giving her time to say no or to push him away. Hope knew this instinctively and raked a hand up into his hair and pulled him closer, making sure he couldn't misinterpret her decision.

That seemed to do the trick because suddenly there wasn't anything slow about what they were doing; it was all heat and need. Hope didn't think it was possible to be pressed so close to another human being. It was almost as if they shared a heartbeat like they were sharing their breath. With the fire heating her back and Beckett heating her front, she was certain her temperature had gone up a hundred degrees.

Her heart was racing and Beckett's hands were roaming up and down her back and everything felt so good and so right that all the negative thoughts about leaving and about Beckett were gone. Instead, Hope felt content and excited, consumed by thoughts of other ways to spend their time tonight that didn't include touring the house or looking at the snow fall.

Hope wasn't the kind of woman who normally went for casual affairs but something about Beckett James called to her and she feared if she didn't act on it, if she didn't do something about it right here, right now, she'd be missing out on something incredible.

He moved his lips from hers and skimmed them over her cheek and down her throat. Her head fell back and she sighed his name, her hands still splayed in his hair. The scene was perfect–the snow, the fire, the possibility of making love in front of it. She said his name again, this time as more of a plea.

Beckett raised his head, his eyes meeting hers. He was as breathless as Hope was as they stared at one another. And as was slowly becoming a habit, he read her mind. "If it were only the two of us here, I wouldn't be stopping. But Norma's here and there's no doubt she'd come out here at some point and I certainly don't want to compromise you like that. You may not believe me, but I respect you too much to do something like that to you."

Hope believed him, but she was too weak to speak.

Taking a step back, Beckett took one of her hands in his. "I'm not sorry we did that, Hope. And I can't say it won't happen again. Soon." And with that, he led her from the room and began the tour of the lodge.

Hope only listened with half an ear at first because all she could think about, all that seemed to fill her mind, were thoughts of more kisses.

Chapter Six

She was beginning to wonder if she had imagined the kiss.

They had toured all ten of the guest suites; each was decorated differently so they had a personality of their own and were all exquisite. She'd already seen the study, the dining room and the kitchen, but on the first floor there was also a large common area that ran the entire length of the back of the house and it was where they were currently standing. The one wall consisted of floor-to-ceiling windows so you could look out on the property.

"It's breathtaking," she said, stepping close to the glass and looking out. The snow wasn't falling nearly as hard as it had earlier. Behind her, Beckett walked to the far corner and threw a switch. She gasped. "Oh, my goodness. It's like…really like a winter wonderland out there."

Outside, woven along the branches of many of the trees, were white twinkly lights. No spotlights, no stadium lights, just thousands upon thousands of little white lights. They seemed to go on for miles. Hope pressed even closer and looked from side to side and couldn't spot where the lights ended. "Oh, Beckett," she sighed, "it's so beautiful. Absolutely beautiful." She almost jumped right out of her skin when he pressed up behind her, his arms wrapping around her waist.

"Are you feeling adventurous?" he murmured against her ear, his breath warm and enticing.

"That depends," she purred, tilting her head in hopes of Beckett's lips coming back to press against her skin. She smiled when his lips trailed a path down the column of her throat. He pulled back way too soon.

"How would you like to go for a walk outside?" he asked softly.

The way Hope was feeling at the moment, she could use the freezing temperatures to cool herself down. There was only one problem. "I don't think my boots have dried out from my earlier adventure. Besides, they're not really meant for the snow."

"Not a problem," he said as he stepped back and took one of her hands in his again. "We have an abundance of boots and coats and hats that we stocked from when we used to open this to the public."

Hope shivered. "I'm not really big on wearing other people's clothes," she said lightly, but Beckett continued walking.

"You won't be. We have a supply closet

downstairs which is full of inventory that was never worn. They're all brand new and still have the tags on them."

It was hard not to question him about why he would hold on to this kind of stuff rather than donate it to a local homeless shelter or even sell it, but she was having too much fun with him to say something that may very well lead to a fight.

They walked down to what would be considered the basement level even though it was above ground. There was a large game room with Ping-Pong tables, air hockey tables, dart boards and pool tables. Hope thought it seemed like a shame that they sat here unused for so many years.

Again, not a topic to bring up right now.

Back in the corner of the room, was the supply closet. Beckett opened the door and reached in and turned on a light. Hope stood there in stunned silence. It was a large walk-in closet and the bars were lined with dozens of coats in seemingly every size and color. On the shelves there were boots that were still in their boxes and in bins on the floor were packages of hats and gloves.

"Take your pick," Beckett said and stepped aside.

"Oh...I don't know. I don't feel right just taking these," she said, still frozen to the spot.

"Hope, it's not a big deal. Please. They've just been sitting here in storage not being used. From what I saw earlier, you didn't have a heavy coat to wear. Or a hat. Or gloves. Come on. Let's find you what you need and go out and walk along under our man-made starry sky."

When he put it like that, Hope couldn't say no. Scanning through the rack, she found a coat in her size while Beckett found her a pair of boots. She went through the bins and found a set of matching hat and gloves and stepped out of the closet. Beckett followed and they walked back up the stairs to the study in silence.

"Why don't you get those on while I go and get mine from my room," he said, motioning to her new boots. "I'll meet you by the back door."

Hope watched him walk away and sighed. Why couldn't he be like this all the time? Like every day all the time? How much better would everyone feel if Beckett loosened up a little bit and actually treated everyone with kindness?

Topic number three to keep to herself. It was almost getting painful at this point.

The boots fit like a dream and as Hope stood up, she couldn't help but admire them. They didn't often get snow in her part of North Carolina so snow boots were never a necessity, but she knew these were top-quality boots and she loved them. As she walked to the back windows, she put on her coat and took the tags off the hat and gloves. Once that was done, she admired the view while she waited.

"How do they fit?" Beckett asked as he walked into the room.

"Perfectly," she said with a smile. Without a word, Beckett held out his hand to her and Hope placed hers in it. They walked toward the back door and she was almost giddy at the thought of walking in the snow under all those twinkly lights.

The cold hit them like a sharp slap in the face when Beckett opened the door, but they quickly donned their hats and gloves and looked at each other with huge smiles as they braced themselves to walk outside.

"You sure you want to do this?" he asked.

Hope stepped around him and felt her feet crunch through the snow that was beginning to harden and ice over. "A little too late to ask," she said impishly. "You're not chickening out are you?"

"Me? Never." He closed the door to the house and took her hand again so they could slowly make their way across the massive back deck to the stairs that would lead them down to the ground.

"Do you have someone to come out here and shovel or do the snow-blower thing or do you do it yourself?" she asked.

Beckett shrugged. "It's been a long time since I've been up here during a storm. Norma usually handles it all so I'm guessing she hires someone. She's great at many things, but I don't see her as the type to be out here clearing the decks, porches, stairs and walkways in the freezing temps."

"That would be something to see." They both laughed and carefully made their way down the dozen steps that led to the ground below. The snow was deep, a little over a foot, so they were going to be walking slowly no matter where they went.

"I can't even remember the last time I went for a walk in the snow," Beckett said, looking around in wonder.

"Me either. You know how it is back home; if

it snows even an inch or two, everything shuts down. I tend to just stay inside and wait it out until it starts to melt."

He chuckled. "When it does snow, I park my car in my garage and then I get to the office and park in that garage, so I pretty much stay out of it. Now I see that it's actually not all that bad."

"Well, I think part of that feeling is because of what you created here. I mean, look around you! The sky is cloudy because of the snow and yet it looks like a clear, star-filled night. You can just barely make out the moon over there." She pointed up toward the sky as some clouds were slowly making their way across the light of the moon. "It's just…amazing. I know I keep saying that but I can't help it. If there were music playing out here, it really would be a winter wonderland."

"Why music?"

"To set the mood even more. Something Christmas-y," she said with a grin. "Nothing with lyrics, something instrumental that just puts you in the mood."

"For what?" he asked thickly from beside her.

Hope blushed at the implications. She glanced over at him. "For the holidays. For Santa. For…dancing in the moonlight." And before she knew it, Beckett had spun her around and she was wrapped in his arms and swaying to an imaginary song in his head.

"You mean like this?" he asked as he rested his forehead against hers.

She sighed and snuggled closer, swaying slowly along with him. "Yes. Exactly like this."

And then suddenly it wasn't an imaginary song in anyone's head, Beckett was humming. Hope smiled against his chest as he hummed out the melody to "Winter Wonderland." And it didn't surprise her one bit to find he did it perfectly. There seemed to be no end to the man's talents.

They stayed like that, with the snow falling around them, swaying under the lights and the moon for a long time. Hope felt Beckett occasionally place a kiss on her temple and she softly hummed her approval. It was perfect. No one had ever done anything like this with her...or for her. If anyone had said she'd be dancing in the middle of a snowstorm, in the moonlight, with a man she couldn't quite figure out, she would have said they were crazy.

Now? Not so much.

Beckett leaned in and rubbed his nose against hers and she shivered. "I think we should go in. You're cold."

"It's cold out," she replied quietly, not wanting this moment to ever end.

"That it is," he chuckled. "But maybe we can get Norma to whip up a little more hot chocolate before she goes to bed."

Well, maybe the moment could end–for now. "That sounds wonderful."

"Your winter wonderland will still be here tomorrow. We can come out again if you'd like and maybe, just maybe, we can arrange some real music."

Reaching up on her tip-toes, Hope kissed him gently on the cheek. "I think tonight's music was wonderful." Then she reached for his hand, and was the one to lead them back to the stairs, up to the deck and back into the house.

～ﾟ～

A girl could get used to this.

That's what was going through Hope's mind as she and Beckett once again sat in front of the fire in the study. They were each in their own chair, but Beckett had positioned them so they were closer together. Norma had prepared hot chocolate for them to warm them up and Hope was feeling very warm and content overall. If only…

"Too bad there isn't a couch here," she said wistfully.

"What?"

"You know, instead of the chairs. It would be nice if there was a big, overstuffed couch here in front of the fire." Looking over at him, Hope couldn't quite determine what he was thinking. His expression was fairly neutral, so that meant there were at least a thousand possibilities of what was going on in his mind.

"Back when we used to have this open as a resort, it was smarter to have more single-seating options in here. Even when we were here as a family, this room wasn't used very much. We tended to either gather down in the game room or in the back room or even the dining room." He shrugged. "I never gave the décor much of a thought for this place. It's just always…been."

"I'm not saying there's anything wrong with

this; these chairs are very comfortable. It's just another possibility, you know, like you have up in some of the suites." Earlier when they were touring the rooms, there were two suites on the top floor that had large sitting areas with a sofa in front of their fireplace. They were the only rooms that seemed to have them and it made for a very inviting space.

Beckett looked over at her and grinned. "Up for moving some furniture?"

Was she? It was getting late, almost ten, and it had been a long and exhausting day. But still...

"Not from the third floor," she said, returning his smile.

"I would never ask that of you." Standing, Beckett placed his mug down and walked across the room.

Hope watched him and there was a doorway she hadn't noticed before. Beckett opened it and stepped inside, pretty much assuring her it wasn't a closet. She stood and followed him and stopped in the doorway.

It was his bedroom.

"Oh," she whispered. It was bigger than all the rooms she'd seen already, even the suites on the top floor. He had a full wall of windows along the back wall that looked out onto the property. How had she not noticed that when they were walking around outside? Everything in this room, however, was new and updated. Fresh paint, new plush carpeting and even without knowing anything about high-end furniture, Hope could tell everything in this room was top of the line.

It wasn't surprising, but she couldn't help but step into the room and look around. Beckett was standing beside a sofa which sat in front of a large stone fireplace that was almost as large as the one in the study.

"I was thinking we could move this out into the study," he said and placed a hand on the sofa.

"What? Why?"

"It sounded like a good idea."

"But...it's already in front of a fireplace. Why move it?"

Slowly, Beckett stepped around the sofa and came to stand in front of her. "Hope, if I had said 'Oh, I have a couch in my bedroom, why don't we go and sit in there?' are you telling me you wouldn't have been offended?"

Would she? Hope wanted to think that on some level she might have been but the reality was that the thought of sitting in front of a fire in Beckett's bedroom was very appealing.

Maybe even too appealing.

Becket stepped in closer and put his hands on her waist. "Hope?"

What could she say? If she said she wouldn't have been offended, did that make her sound too anxious? Too easy? On the other hand, if she said that she would have been, then they'd go back to sitting in their separate chairs and that was just...well, it wasn't the most exciting option she could think of.

"I...," she looked up and met his gaze. Beckett's eyes were dark, his expression serious and if possible, Hope was beyond caring about everything she knew about him before. She wanted to live right here, right now with the man she was coming to know tonight. "I wouldn't have minded."

A slow smile crept across Beckett's face as his head lowered toward hers. "We could always start a fire in here."

"I think we already have," she whispered and went up on her toes to close the distance between them.

There was no slow start to the kiss, once their lips touched it was explosive. Hope was surprised the fireplace didn't simultaneously burst into flames from the heat they were generating. Beckett's arms banded around her middle as her own wound up around his shoulders as they pressed closer together.

There were no warning bells in her head. Her subconscious was suspiciously quiet. If Hope had to venture a guess, she would have to say that this was right. Her being here with Beckett–in his home, in his bedroom–was exactly where she was supposed to be. And as her hands raked up into his raven-colored hair and she heard a growl from deep in his throat, she'd have to say that Beckett felt the same way.

Over and over his lips moved over hers. They kept moving against one another as if trying to find a position that was perfect for them. Beckett began to move them toward the couch and once they were beside it, he carefully began to sit down and pulled Hope with him until she was straddling his lap. And still they didn't break the kiss. Hope wiggled in his lap and that's when she felt it, the proof that he was just as turned on as she was. Beckett's strong hands grasped her hips and held her firmly against him and Hope almost cried out at the contact.

It was exactly the position she had been trying to get to.

When they finally broke apart, they were breathless. Hope slowly licked at her lips and smiled when Beckett growled again. She leaned forward, her forehead against his and sighed. "What are we doing?" she asked quietly and then could have kicked herself. She would have been perfectly okay moving forward without uttering a single word. They had a terrible tendency to argue as soon as one of them spoke.

"I thought we were just going to move some furniture, but I like what we're doing way better," he teased softly and placed a gentle kiss on the tip of her nose.

Hope chuckled. "Beckett…"

"I know, I know." Reaching up, he cupped her face in his hands and put a little space between them. "I want you, Hope. I've wanted you since the first moment I saw you." He paused and studied her face. "I never expected to have the chance to, not after the way things were going back home. I knew how you felt about me, the real me, and I knew if you ever found out the truth, you'd hate me. And you did."

"Beckett…"

"It's the truth, Hope," he said simply. "But you're here now." His hands made a slow path across her cheeks, down her throat, over her shoulders, down her arms until they were resting on her hips again. "And I really want you to get to know me, not the person you think you know or the person you've heard other people talk about, but me."

"I want that," she admitted. "And I think you know I want you too. It was the same for me. That night at the office was a great night for me. Meeting you wasn't something I ever expected and I was pretty devastated earlier today when I realized who you are." She swallowed hard. "But...I'm willing to take a chance here and not let what I thought I knew about you affect what I'm feeling about you right now." Her eyes met his and held.

"Are you sure?"

Hope nodded. "I don't know what's going to happen tomorrow, but I know how I feel right now, Beckett, and what I want."

"And what's that?" he asked thickly.

"I know I don't want to move furniture," she said with a sexy grin. "At least, I don't want to move it to another room. I'm pretty content with staying right here in this one and seeing how we can maybe make some of this furniture move."

For a minute, she thought she'd been too bold, too obvious and maybe Beckett had gotten turned off by her silly banter. She was just about to apologize, to try to take it all back when she noticed the heat in his gaze. "Beckett?"

Wrapping one arm around her waist and the other under her bottom, Beckett stood with Hope in his arms. Without a word, he strode over and shut the bedroom door. The only light in the room was coming from the twinkly lights that were still on outside. He walked them over to his bed and lay her down on top of it before taking a step back.

Hope began to squirm under the intensity of his gaze. Never in her life had a man looked at her like this. Boldly, she reached out a hand for him and smiled when he accepted it and came down beside her on the bed. "That's better," she said and cupped his face in her hand.

"I can't believe you're really here," Beckett said, his own hand now skimming her face.

"I really am."

"If you'd like, I can light a fire in here. This one's a gas fireplace so I only have to flip a switch."

As much as she hated the thought of him getting up, the thought of the fire was a little too enticing. "I think I'd like that." She watched as Beckett got up and walked over to the stone fireplace and flipped a switch that seemed to be hidden within the stone and then he was back beside her and then rolling onto his side and pressing closer to her.

"We don't have to do anything you don't want to do," he said, his voice low. "I'd be happy just to have you here beside me so I could hold you all night."

And just like that, Hope knew she was lost.

There was no doubt he was as turned on as she was and there was no doubt that two minutes ago, they were ready to get naked and devour one another. But to hear him say he wouldn't mind just holding her, that meant more than anything else Beckett could have said. And looking up into his eyes, Hope knew he was speaking the truth.

"I want you to hold me, Beckett," she said slowly, "but not until you're done making love to me."

The smile that washed over his face was one of wonder and relief. "My pleasure."

Hope felt positively boneless.

And in the best way possible.

True to his word, Beckett was holding her close–her head nestled on his shoulder, her hand on his bare chest. She sighed with contentment and smiled when she felt him kiss the top of her head. They had been lying there like this in the firelight without saying a word for quite some time. For Hope, she was quiet because there were no words to describe exactly what she was feeling. Everything she and Beckett had done in this room, in this bed, had been mind blowing.

It wasn't simply about orgasms, although there were many; it was about the way he made her feel inside. Every touch of his hands, every move of his body was everything she'd ever dreamed of in a lover. It was as if he knew her, really knew her, because it seemed to be Beckett's sole intention to please her. Any time she'd tried to reciprocate, he'd somehow maneuvered them until she was crying out with pleasure.

Definitely not a bad way to spend the night.

They'd made love for what seemed like hours and Beckett's eyes had never left her face. He'd already told her how expressive her face was but now, after watching his just as intently, she could say the same for him. This wasn't only about physical release, Hope felt like she could see clear to Beckett's soul.

And it scared the heck out of her.

∽ల౿∾

The snow had finally tapered off and the skies were clearing and if he was guessing correctly, Beckett would say that the moon was fully visible now. He glanced over at the clock and saw it was after one in the morning. Hope was asleep in his arms and he closed his eyes and just enjoyed the feeling of having her there.

He wasn't lying earlier when he admitted that he'd wanted her ever since he first saw her. The problem was that he knew how much she hated him. Never in his life had Beckett had to lie about who he was, but with Hope, it was the only way for her to give him a chance. Women threw themselves at him all the time, and for the most part, Beckett was flattered by the attention. He'd grown up as a shy, computer geek and to see and have all kinds of beautiful women vying for his attention was a real ego boost for a long time.

Then he realized it wasn't him they were throwing themselves at, but his money.

But with Hope, knowing how things started out with them and seeing how they were right now, he knew that his money had nothing to do with it. She was here because of him. Beckett. Not G.B. James or James Enterprises, but just him. His heart seemed to lurch at the thought of it. Without conscious thought, he held her a little tighter.

This was something he never did, spend the entire night with a woman in his own bed. Hell, who was he kidding? He never spent an entire night in any bed with any woman. Because his relationships tended to lean toward the superficial, it wasn't unusual to get up and leave once they were done. And Beckett never–*never!*–had a woman back to his place and certainly not in his bed.

Until Hope.

Why it was her? Beckett couldn't say. The attraction was instantaneous, but even when she mentioned her dislike of the head of the company, Beckett didn't take it so much as a challenge but more of a desire to get to know her. It was never about changing her mind. Well, maybe it was a little, but the more time they spent together, and it wasn't much, it became more important for him to be the person who he used to be, the person who he truly wanted to be and, deep down, still was. And would probably still continue to be if the population as a whole wasn't out to try to get something from him every time he blinked.

Employees wanted favors–extra time for projects, to leave early, to come in late…the list was endless. Friends had started to look to him for some of the perks her could afford–VIP seats to concerts and sporting events, entry into the newest clubs and restaurants. Some had even asked for cash to start up businesses or to buy a car or a house.

But the worst had been his own family.

When his father passed away, as the oldest child in the family, Beckett had inherited the company his grandfather began more than forty years ago. It wasn't only because he was the oldest that he got it, however, it was because he was the only one in the family who actually had taken an interest in it and had worked there.

For as long as he could remember, Beckett used to love to go and tour the hotels with his grandfather. They'd walk the properties, inspect the rooms and talk about where to make improvements that were needed, but most of all, his grandfather had taught him how to see the potential in a property and how to turn one around.

Luckily, Beckett had a natural inclination toward business management and it had helped him to take James Enterprises from being a little-known name in the hospitality industry to one in the top ten. As the success of the company grew with Beckett at the helm, his siblings had suddenly started to take interest.

Or so he'd thought.

First, his brother Logan had come to see him. Beckett had always thought they were close but Logan never wanted to be involved in the business. He thought hotels and hotel management wasn't a masculine kind of career and instead had become a mechanic. Logan presented a very loosely planned idea of having mechanics on-site at some of the hotels.

Like the ones Logan lived near.

He'd be the resident mechanic and if a guest was having car trouble, Logan would be given the business. All he wanted in return, besides all the money for the repairs, was for Beckett to set him up with a state-of-the-art custom garage and a list of all the hotel guests so Logan could reach out and market to them.

Except, he expected Beckett's marketing department for the hotels to handle that for him.

Beckett had quickly told him there was no way the company was going to do any of those things and Logan had stormed off while calling him every name in the book and telling him to go to hell.

No one else in the family mentioned it, but there was one less person at Christmas that year.

Not long after Christmas, his sister Julie had invited him to dinner to meet her fiancé Colton. His sister was always his weak spot. Because she was the baby of the family and she reminded him so much of his mother, Beckett always seemed to overcompensate wherever she was concerned. And he never minded doing it. Why? Because Julie always seemed to feel bad about the things Beckett did for her and she never asked for anything.

Until that night.

Colton started his sales pitch as soon as Beckett had walked in the door. He'd barely had his coat off before the man started asking about the hotels and the supplier for clothes with the hotel logos on them. Seriously? Beckett had played it cool and tried to get a feel for where it was all leading. Then Colton mentioned how he did silk screening on t-shirts out of his garage and thought he'd be the perfect guy to do apparel for the hotels. When Beckett had asked him how he expected to do that kind of quantity of merchandise, Julie chimed in by saying Beckett could set them up with a printing shop.

Um…no.

And that was the last time he'd seen or spoken to his sister.

Hope hummed in her sleep and Beckett placed a light kiss on her forehead. It was because of his family that he didn't extend favors to anyone and he certainly didn't like to mix business with his employees' family members.

He wasn't stupid. He remembered Ted coming to him with Hope's proposal to do a small café in one of the newer hotels they were opening in the Raleigh area and Beckett had turned her down. She had a solid business plan with the exception of not having enough startup capital and if she and Ted weren't related, he actually might have considered it. But he'd learned the hard way that you can't mix the two, ever. Eventually, things were going to go south and it was just easier to have no real connection to your tenants, employees, suppliers…any of them.

Of course it meant that he was cutting himself off from a lot of people. To date, James Enterprises owned over one hundred resorts worldwide. The office in Raleigh housed over five hundred employees. And the amount of suppliers they had on the payroll was endless. Suffice it to say, he kept his distance from them all for the sake of self-preservation.

Until now.

What would happen tomorrow? What would

happen when, and if, Ted returned? Would Hope expect him to give her brother his job back? Would she expect him to reconsider her business proposal? For a brief moment, his mind filled with negative scenarios and then he felt her lips softly kissing his chest.

Beckett could admit he didn't know everything there was to know about Hope Cooper, but what he did know was that she was fiercely independent and didn't look for handouts. She'd created her own business when most people would have been satisfied collecting a paycheck for having to do an easy job. She was generous to a fault and if anything, she encouraged her brother to stand up for himself rather than sitting back and letting others dictate to him how to live.

No, Hope wasn't going to make any demands on him, of that he was certain. But there was no doubt things were going to change once her brother showed up. The weather gave them a slight reprieve, a chance for them to actually get to know one another and to explore the relationship they'd begun weeks ago. He knew she was going to leave and so was he. They both had lives back in Raleigh and this was just a chance opportunity.

He just didn't want her to leave so soon.

A yawn escaped before he could stop it. He needed sleep. It had been a long day and even though he normally didn't sleep very much, for the first time in a long time, his mind wasn't going a million miles an hour with work stuff. He was kind of feeling mellow, relaxed.

"Beckett?" she whispered in the dark and

immediately, his body seemed to rejuvenate itself. Hope's hands began to wander, along with her mouth, and this time, Beckett let himself simply lie back and let her lead.

༺༺༻

The next time Hope woke up, she was alone.

The room was bright due to the sun being up and reflecting against the crisp whiteness of the snow. She slowly sat up in the bed and looked around the room. The clock on the bedside table showed it was after nine. She couldn't even remember the last time she had let herself sleep in.

A little thankful that she was alone, Hope climbed out of the bed and quickly gathered her clothes that were scattered all over the floor and got dressed. She had no idea where Beckett was but hopefully she'd be able to leave the room and go upstairs to her own so she could shower and change before seeing him.

Or anyone.

Slowly opening the door, she looked out into the study and didn't see him. Feeling like she was a spy in stealth mode, she made her way across the room, out to the entryway and up the stairs and breathed a sigh of relief when she made it to her room without seeing either Beckett or Norma. Her heart was beating rapidly and she leaned her back against the door and slid to the ground and wondered what she had done.

She had slept with the enemy.

That thought immediately felt wrong and she

shook her head. Beckett wasn't the enemy and she needed to stop thinking of him like that. He ran a huge company that spanned who-knew how many places and he had a right to run it any way he wanted or needed to. Hope was ashamed at the way she had judged him all these years. Now that she was getting to know him, she knew there was more to him than just being the head of a major corporation.

He was a man who she enjoyed being with.

A man who made her smile.

A man she was falling in love with.

Uh-oh...

That was the first time she allowed herself to even think such a thing but now that she had, Hope knew it to be true. She was falling in love with Beckett. Not Ted's boss or the CEO, but the man. *Wow.* Now what was she supposed to do?

A man like Beckett was probably used to dating debutantes and socialites, not computer geeks who played video games and went to Comic-Con. Yikes. She was in so much trouble and way out of her league. Jumping to her feet, Hope went and pulled her phone out of her purse and tried calling Ted. She needed him to come and get her no matter what, before she made an even bigger fool out of herself and told Beckett how she felt.

Of course the rat-fink didn't answer his phone. She tried dialing Merry's number but it went to voicemail too. At least Merry had an excuse. Ted, on the other hand, was going to be on the receiving end of a major hissy fit when he finally decided to show his face.

With nothing left to do, Hope tossed her phone back in her purse and went and took her shower. Thirty minutes later, she felt a little more in control of herself. A hot shower, fresh clothes, and no more morning breath meant she could face the day with at least a little of confidence.

When she arrived down in the kitchen, she found Norma sitting and having a cup of tea and reading a book. "Good morning," she said shyly and smiled when Norma smiled.

"Oh, good morning, Hope. I trust you slept well," Norma said as she stood and walked over to the stove. "Would you like tea or coffee? There's juice in the refrigerator if you'd prefer."

"Um…juice would be fine." She turned to get it herself, but Norma playfully swatted her away and told her to sit down. "You don't have to wait on me. Seriously. I don't mind getting things for myself."

"Nonsense. You're a guest here."

"Not really. More like an accidental tourist."

Norma laughed. "Either way, you're here and I don't mind waiting on you. I baked some muffins this morning. I've got blueberry and banana chocolate chip and…"

"Ooo…banana chocolate chip sounds wonderful!"

"Believe me, they are. Those are Beckett's favorite too."

It was starting to get a little eerie how much they had in common and how in sync they were with one another. "Do you think I could just have a glass of milk with that instead?"

Norma laughed again.

"What? What's so funny?"

"That's exactly how he has his too!" She shook her head as she poured Hope a glass of milk and then went and put a muffin on a plate. "I'm just going to warm this up for a few seconds in the microwave. They should still be a little warm, but…just in case."

"Thank you." When the timer beeped, Norma took the plate and placed it on the table along with the glass of milk. Hope thanked her again. "So, any update on the roads? Are they cleared and open?"

"Actually, I didn't watch the news this morning. We have a television in the common area and down in the game room…or even up in your room but I think most of the morning news shows are over by now. Maybe you can ask Beckett to go online and check for you."

Sure, that was one way she could go but right now she still didn't feel confident in facing Beckett. What they had shared last night left her feeling weak and needy and totally wanting more. She knew he'd see it in her face immediately. For now, she was happy to hide out in the kitchen behind this softball-sized muffin and stay uninformed about the road conditions.

"I hope you don't mind, but I moved all of your cookie tins to the dining room on the buffet. This way they're accessible if either you or Beckett want them."

"You're welcome to have some too, Norma. There's obviously enough for a small army there."

They laughed. "I've been baking for weeks and as much as I enjoy it and I love all the cookies I make, I really don't want to take any back home with me."

"I'm sure Beckett wouldn't mind you leaving some with him."

"Leaving some of what?" he asked as he strode into the room.

At just the sight of him, Hope felt her heart go crazy and her cheeks heat.

"Cookies. I told Hope I moved all of her cookies to the dining room and she said she didn't want to take them back home with her. I figured you wouldn't mind her leaving some behind for you."

Beckett smiled at Norma and then at Hope and in that minute she knew…he knew.

And there wasn't a muffin big enough to hide behind.

Chapter *Seven*

"This is surreal."

"I know."

"I don't think I'll ever be able to go back to the way things were before."

"I imagine it would be difficult."

"I think I'm going to...*damn it, Beckett!* You were supposed to be on lookout! Now I've gotten shot!" Hope did her best to maneuver her character around, but she was quickly losing life. "One thing! You had *one* thing to do!"

Beckett couldn't help but laugh. Hope had said she enjoyed playing video games. He just didn't think she took them quite so seriously. "Okay, okay. Sorry. I got distracted."

"Yeah, great," she muttered. "Just who I need on my team, a guy who's easily distracted."

"You know this isn't real, right?"

She shot him a furious look. "What is the point

in playing if you're not going to take it seriously?"

He knew laughing at her again wouldn't bode well for him, but he couldn't help it. "Hope, this is supposed to be fun. We were supposed to be relaxing and having a good time."

"Fun? You thought playing a shooter game was fun? If that's what you were looking for you should have pulled out a Disney game or something with Legos." She tossed her controller down and stood up. "I'm going to get something to drink."

She was mad and Beckett thought she was adorable. Who would have thought that women got as involved with these games as men did? *Learn something new every day*, he thought to himself and caught her before she reached the stairs. "Hey," he turned her around and wrapped his arms around her. "I'm sorry. I didn't think you'd be so competitive. I thought we were just playing around."

Unfortunately, that seemed to make her angrier.

"I mean…you take it very seriously and I usually don't. I'm sorry. I didn't mean to upset you."

Looking up at him, Hope seemed to relax. "No, you're right. I take it too seriously. It's why Ted refuses to play any games with me. Well, that and the fact that I kick his butt at all of them." She chuckled. "I'm sorry. I shouldn't have gotten so mad."

"So I'm forgiven?" he asked as one corner of his mouth began to twitch.

She sighed dramatically. "I guess so." And then she smiled as Beckett pulled her in and held her close.

It was the first time he'd allowed himself to touch her since he climbed from the bed earlier that morning. Actually, he hadn't wanted to leave the bed, or Hope, but his mind was racing with several ideas for the project he was supposed to be working on and he had some calls to make to start getting things in motion. Just because Beckett knew he was going to work through Christmas didn't guarantee the rest of the world would. It was better to get things moving before the holiday actually hit so that by the time he got back to the office, along with the masses, he wouldn't be behind schedule too much.

"I think I'm a little hungry," Hope said, looking up at him. "I hate to ask Norma to make something for us. Can't we just go up and raid the fridge?"

"Norma doesn't mind preparing a meal, Hope. Trust me. And even if you think you could just go up and do that, she'll stop you. I know. She's caught me making midnight snacks that she swatted my hand over and ended up making herself."

"Wow. She's strict."

"It's her kitchen and she's very protective of it," he said with a teasing glint in his eyes.

"I'll have to remember that. So what do you say? Should we go up and ask her about lunch?"

"In a minute," he said and bent forward and kissed her. It was slow and leisurely and Beckett sighed when Hope pressed closer and wrapped her arms around him. She was quickly becoming addictive to him. He was never the kind of man who showed affection outside of the bedroom, but where she was concerned, Beckett knew he'd want to touch her, kiss her and let everyone know she was his no matter where they were. When he lifted his head, he was pleased to see she was just as dazed as he was.

"That was nice," she said softly. "I was beginning to think last night was just my imagination."

He grinned. True, there hadn't been any pillow talk this morning, and he knew that it was probably wrong of him to leave her alone, but it couldn't be helped. Beckett wasn't used to taking other people's feelings into consideration in most things and he realized now how it could have looked to Hope to have her wake up in his room and have him be gone.

"Sorry about that," he said and skimmed a finger along her cheek. "You were sleeping so peacefully and I had a couple of calls to make. Then one thing led to another and…"

"It's all right, Beckett. I didn't expect you to stop working because I'm here. If anything, I'm surprised you're not working more. I know Ted's leaving put a major crimp in what you needed to get done, but I certainly didn't expect you to completely stop and spend all of your time with me."

"I enjoy spending time with you," he said simply.

And she smiled. "And I enjoy spending time with you too. I just don't want you to think that you *have* to spend time with me. It's okay for you to go and work. I'm sure the plows are out and about and with any luck, I'll be out of your hair by tomorrow."

That thought did not sit well with him. "Have

you heard from Ted?"

She shook her head. "He's still not answering and neither is Merry. I'm seriously getting pissed. It's one thing to take off and steal my car, it's quite another to keep ignoring my calls."

"There's no hurry for you to leave, Hope," Beckett said and hoped he didn't sound as desperate as he felt.

Hope arched a brow at him. "It's not that I'm in a hurry, I just…I know you came up here with an agenda and I hate that I'm the reason it got ruined."

An idea began to take root in Beckett's mind.

"What? What's that grin about?" she asked, a slow smile crossing her own face.

"What? What grin?"

"You look like the cat who swallowed the canary."

"I was just thinking maybe…you might want to make it up to me."

She stared at him for a long moment and then seemed to catch on. "Make it up to you? You mean for messing up your perfectly crafted schedule?"

Beckett nodded.

"Hmm…what did you have in mind?" she said and slowly ran a hand up his chest and up into his hair.

"Did I happen to mention the things that used to go on down here in the supply closet?"

Hope shook her head.

"It was famous for being the spot where people would go to fool around."

"Did you ever use the closet to fool around

with the female guests?"

"A time or two."

Hope laughed. "Somehow, I'm thinking it happened more than that."

"A gentleman never tells."

That made her laugh even harder and then she looked over her shoulder toward the closet door. "I have to admit, I've never fooled around in a supply closet, especially not when there are ten empty beds in the house."

That made Beckett stop and think for a minute. Rather than speak, his hands went down and cupped her bottom and lifted. "Wrap your legs around me," he said gruffly. She complied. "We'll get around to the beds later. This is much closer. Saves time."

"You are a very efficient man," she purred against his throat and trailed kisses there.

"Sweetheart, you have no idea." But he planned on showing her just how efficient he could be.

❧

After dinner, Hope was wandering around the house looking for something to do. Norma had gone to bed early with a headache and Beckett said he had some calls to make. She knew she had said she didn't mind that he worked, but right now she wouldn't mind some company.

Standing on the main floor at the base of the stairs she contemplated her options. There was always the game room downstairs. Beckett proved that even though the place wasn't used very often, he kept all the gaming consoles and game selections up-to-date. It wouldn't be a hardship to go down there and veg out on the couch for an hour or two with a game.

And yet she didn't go.

There was the possibility of reading by the fire in the study. She had her Kindle with her and Beckett had started a fire up earlier. She could curl up in a chair and get caught up on her reading and maybe make herself some cocoa and a plate of cookies to nibble on while she read.

And yet that didn't seem appealing either.

Walking into the dining room, she did help herself to a couple of brownie crisps and sat down at the table with a sigh. "I should have brought my computer with me. At least I could be working." But even that didn't do anything for her. "Bored, bored, bored…"

Off in the distance, she heard Beckett's voice. His office was here on the main floor down the hall from the dining room, but he seemed to be talking rather loudly. Unable to help herself, she wiped away the crumbs from her snack and carefully ventured down the hall.

The door wasn't open enough for her to see Beckett, but enough that she could see a sliver of the room and hear him speaking forcefully to whoever was on the other end of the phone.

"That's not an excuse, damn it!" he yelled. "We had an agreement, you broke it and now you're going to try to lay the blame on me? I don't think so."

Hope's heart raced and part of her wanted to

just turn and walk away and forget what she was hearing but she couldn't seem to make her feet cooperate.

"Yes, I'm aware of the time restrictions. I was the one who put them in place. They're there for a reason. You wanted to do business with me and you told me you were confident in being able to meet the guidelines." He paused. "So then what you're saying to me is that you're a liar, is that it?" Another pause. "I believe we're done here."

And then there was silence.

Without the good old days where phones were put on a cradle that you could slam for dramatic effect, Hope had no idea if Beckett was still on the phone or if the person he was talking with was taking their turn at talking. Either way, she knew it was wrong to stay there and eavesdrop so she turned and walked back toward the dining room.

"Hope?"

Busted. Slowly she turned around. "Hi," she said weakly.

"Is everything okay?" he asked, concern etching his brow.

"I…I was um…I was having a couple of cookies and I heard you yelling. I guess I should ask if everything's okay with you." Her heart was racing and she silently prayed he wasn't going to be angry about her being there.

He sighed and leaned against the wall, raking a hand through his hair. "Just dealing with a difficult subcontractor. We've got renovations going on at our hotel in Florida near the panhandle and we wanted everything done in time for New Year's."

"And it's not going to be?"

He shook his head. "He didn't take into account the holidays and how he had given most of his crew the time off. Now he's shorthanded and expects me to be sympathetic. We've got the ballroom booked for New Year's Eve and not being completed isn't an option."

"So what are you going to do?"

"Fire him."

"Fire him?" she repeated incredulously. "But...but...it's Christmas! Surely you're going to run into the same problem with other contractors!"

Beckett shrugged. "With the right incentive, I'll get a full crew in to finish the job."

"You mean pay a bunch of workers to miss Christmas?" she asked sarcastically, crossing her arms across her chest.

"Hope..."

"You know what...just forget it. It's none of my business." Turning around, she walked away and was surprised when Beckett didn't try to stop her. She made it all the way to the study when she realized she didn't want to be there, or here or...anywhere. With no other choice, she walked up the stairs to her room and shut the door.

For the life of her, Hope couldn't say why she was so surprised. Disappointed, yes. Surprised, no. For years she had known all about G.B. James. Just because she now knew him personally as Beckett didn't mean he was a different person. Her first impression of him had sadly been correct.

And it depressed her.

It was too early to go to bed but that didn't stop

her from going over to her suitcase and pulling out the oversized t-shirt she brought with her to sleep in. Going through her night-time ritual of getting ready for bed did little to relax her. When she was done, Hope walked over to her purse and pulled out her phone and prayed either Ted or Merry would answer their phones.

Ted didn't.

Merry did.

"Merry!" she said and almost sagged with relief. "Hey, it's Hope! How are you feeling?"

"Sore," she said, "but I'm home and my folks are here and Ted's here taking care of me so I'm fine. How are you doing?"

How was she doing? Was Merry serious? "Me? Oh, I'm…fine. Snowed in up in the mountains but other than that, I'm fine. Listen, is…is Ted there?"

"He is. Hold on a sec."

Hope wanted to scream. Her brother hadn't even bothered to try to come back for her! It was official. She was going to kill him. Slowly. Painfully. She would…

"Hey, Hope," Ted said weakly as he got on the phone.

"Oh, hey, Ted," Hope said, through clenched teeth. "Long time no see."

"How…how are you doing?"

"How do you think I'm doing, you inconsiderate jackass? You stole my car! You left me here with your boss! In a blizzard! I tried to walk to a hotel and fell down a snowy embankment and nearly got frostbite!"

"Why? Why would you do that? Mr. James has an entire house of unused rooms."

"By the way, I'm fine. Thanks for asking." Sometimes her brother was completely obtuse. All the more reason to strangle him and put him out of his misery. When he didn't say anything, she snapped. "That's it? That's all you have to say? Are you for real right now? Did you honestly believe I would stay here willingly? What were you thinking?"

"I know, I know...I panicked. I knew if we both walked out, I could kiss my job goodbye and..."

"Your job's already gone, Ted. He told you before you walked out. I just can't believe you dumped my stuff in the snow and took off!"

"At the time it made perfect sense. You'd stay and work with him and then I'd come back."

"But you didn't come back!" Hope yelled. "Obviously you're still in Raleigh at Merry's house and I'm still here. Care to explain that one?"

"She was coming home today and I wanted to be the one to bring her here."

"Her parents are there, Ted. It wasn't necessary for you to do that. Or maybe you could have done it and then gotten your sorry butt back in my car and drove here to get me!" Her head was pounding now and she wanted to throw something. "When are you coming back here? Can you be here in the morning?"

"I...I don't know. The roads aren't great and..."

"Theodore Alexander Cooper, you had *better*

get here tomorrow morning and get me! Do you understand? If you don't, I will file a police report for a stolen vehicle and send the cops directly to your house!"

"Okay, don't be so dramatic. All I'm saying is…"

"No! You're not allowed to say anything anymore. *Ever!* You totally screwed me here, Ted. I went out of my way to help you and Merry and what you did to me was completely uncalled for."

"Are you helping Mr. James with the project?"

Hope pulled the phone away from her ear and pretended to choke it with both hands. "You're kidding, right? He's not my boss! I'm not his employee! I don't work for him and I don't want to. There was never a possibility of me doing your job."

"So…so what have you been doing? Just…hanging around and stuff? It's beautiful up there. I kind of wish I would have had some more time to look around."

It was obvious that aliens had abducted Ted and sucked his brain out because there was no way she was having this conversation with a sane, rational man. "Tell you what, you come and get me in the morning and I'll take you on a tour of the property. Deal?"

"Hope…"

"I'm done talking about this," she interrupted. "Be here in the morning, Ted. I'm not kidding."

"Fine," he said almost belligerently.

"Excuse me, but what right do you have to an attitude?"

"I don't want to go all the way back up there, Hope. I'm going to have to face Mr. James and know that I let him down and listen to him berate me and know that my job is officially gone."

"It's gone whether you come back here or not. You knew that."

"I was hoping to give him time to cool down. I thought if you could help him with some of the stuff…"

"Not talking about this," she snapped. "Be here in the morning, Ted. Or else." And she hung up. Tossing her phone back in her purse, Hope flopped down on the bed and growled with frustration. "When did my brother become such an idiot?"

Now she was wound up, bored, and felt like a caged animal all at the same time. Maybe a couple of hours of video games where she could beat the crap out of someone wasn't such a bad idea. Standing, she went over to her suitcase and pulled out a band for her hair and put it up in a ponytail. She was just about to walk out of the room when she looked down.

No pants.

Ugh. While she knew Beckett had already seen her completely undressed, it still didn't seem right to go prancing around the house in just a t-shirt. Looking over her shoulder she thought about putting her jeans back on and that was just so not going to happen. The only thing worse than that would be being forced to put her bra back on.

"Reading it is," she sighed.

Settling on a romantic suspense story that she

had heard about, she got herself comfortable and did her best to clear her mind and get into the story.

She wasn't sure how much time had passed when there was a light knock on the bedroom door. "Come in," she said absently. The heroine in the book was out walking by herself and was about to be abducted and Hope was on the edge of her seat.

"Hey," Beckett said softly from the doorway. "Can I come in?"

"Your house," she replied, eyes never leaving the screen.

"I was looking all over for you. I figured you'd be downstairs in the game room working on world domination."

"Uh-huh." Didn't he see she was busy? Wait…how could the heroine *not* hear that many people moving around behind her on what was supposed to be a deserted street?

"Are you all right?"

She nodded and then gasped as she read that it wasn't an abductor following the heroine, but her long-lost father! Where did he come from?

"Hope?"

With a sigh of frustration, she put her Kindle down and looked up. "What?" Her impatience was obvious.

Beckett walked over and sat down on the corner of the bed. "I just wanted to make sure, you know, that you were all right."

Hope looked over at the clock beside the bed and saw it was after nine. It took him over two hours to do that? "I'm fine," she lied.

"Are you sure? Because I know things got a

little…I mean, I know it bothered you earlier, hearing me on the phone."

She held up her hand to stop him. "Yeah, it bothered me but I'm over it. Like I said, it's your business and none of mine. You need to do what you need to do. Obviously you know what you're doing because your company is a success. I mean, what do I know? I work for myself and I have all of twelve customers. It doesn't take a genius to figure out who's smarter."

Beckett just sat there and studied her for a moment. "I was wondering if you wanted to go for a walk with me. I wanted to go outside and get some air. I thought it would be nice for us to go together."

He sounded so sweet and sincere. Hopeful. Unfortunately, she wasn't in the mood for any of it. If she wasn't willing to put on pants to go down two flights of stairs to play video games, she sure as heck wasn't about to put on layers of clothes to go and walk in the snow when it was below freezing outside.

"Thanks, but I'm not really in the mood to go outside. I'm in the middle of a good book." God she sounded lame. And bitchy. She prided herself on not being that kind of girl and yet she pretty much had a shining red "B" emblazoned on her chest.

"Oh. Okay. Sorry," he said and stood up. "I didn't mean to disturb you." Walking over to the door, he placed a hand on the handle and turned back toward her. "Good night, Hope."

She couldn't even bring herself to look at him.

"Good night." The door closed quietly and it wasn't until she heard the click that she was able to move. But once she did, she turned off the Kindle and slouched down on the bed.

What was she going to do? Beckett was who he was. She didn't understand the way he did business but who's to say that he was wrong? He was completely within his rights to fire a contractor who couldn't make a deadline. The fact that it was happening over Christmas should be irrelevant. Was she being unfair? Too judgmental?

Maybe.

Was there a possibility she could learn to accept his way of doing business without wanting to correct him or tell him how he was behaving badly?

Maybe.

Did she really want to be sitting in bed reading a book when she could be spending time with Beckett walking in the winter wonderland he had on the property before she had to return to her regular, sucky life?

No.

Jumping up from the bed, she quickly dressed– except for the bra–and took her hair out of the ponytail and shook it out. A light outside her window caught her eye and she ran over and saw that Beckett had turned on all the twinkly lights. Craning her neck, she looked around a bit and found him standing out on the back deck.

Deciding it didn't matter that she had on no makeup or that her hair wasn't fully under control, she traipsed down the stairs and ran toward the common area. She found her boots, coat and hat by the back door and quickly donned them. Bending down, she scooped up her gloves and walked out the door.

Beckett stood with his back to her, leaning on the rail and looking out onto the massive expanse of property. She came up beside him and took in the view. With the moon out and actual stars in the sky, it was very bright and incredibly beautiful, but very cold. She shivered and without a word, Beckett moved and came to stand behind her as he wrapped his arms around her waist.

"I was hoping you'd change your mind," he said quietly.

"Sorry about that. I was having a bad night."

"And I'm sorry about that. I didn't mean to upset you."

Hope shrugged. "It wasn't just you. I finally got my brother on the phone." Beckett stiffened behind her. "I think I may seriously have to kill him when he gets here tomorrow."

"He's coming here? Tomorrow? When?"

"I don't know a specific time. I told him to be here in the morning. He claimed he didn't come back today like he promised because the doctors released Merry from the hospital and he wanted to be the one to take her home and he thought the roads were still messed up."

"And you don't believe him?"

She shook her head. "I think he's too scared to come back here."

"Of me or you?" Beckett asked with a chuckle.

"It's a coin toss," she said and sighed. "He actually thought I would stay here and do his job so

173

you'd reconsider firing him. Can you believe that?"

"Nothing surprises me anymore, Hope. I'm immune to it."

She desperately wanted Beckett to elaborate, but not right now. Right now the night was peaceful and beautiful and magical looking. Why ruin it? "I don't even want to talk about it anymore. I was pissed off and I shouldn't have taken it out on you."

He placed a gentle kiss on her temple before taking a step back and taking one of her hands in his. "Come on. Let's go and walk around. We have actual stars and moonlight tonight."

"I know," she said excitedly. "I love it." They were just about to walk down the steps when Beckett stopped and reached over to the wall and flipped a switch. "What was that for?"

He shrugged and led her back toward the steps. "Careful. I salted the steps after I cleared them earlier, but they can still be slick."

"When did you come out and clear them?"

"This morning when you were still sleeping."

The memory of waking up in Beckett's bed made her smile. "That's quite the invigorating way to start the day. I imagine it was pretty darn cold out."

"About as cold as it is now," he said casually as they walked along a path that led into the woods.

Hope noticed that although it wasn't completely cleared, there was a path in the snow and it was leading to...wait. She turned and looked up at Beckett. "Am I seeing things?"

"That depends? What do you think you're

seeing?"

"A gazebo."

"You're not seeing things."

"What's a gazebo doing in the woods?"

They approached it and Hope saw it was completely cleared off and the roof was covered in the same white lights that coated the trees. They walked up the steps and Beckett took the opportunity to turn Hope in his arms and pull her close. She was just about to ask him again about the gazebo when she suddenly heard the music start, Bing Crosby's "Winter Wonderland" to be exact.

"Oh," she sighed and smiled. "Oh that's nice."

Together they swayed to the music. "I thought you'd prefer this to my humming. I know I do."

"I didn't think you'd have any Christmas music."

"Why? Because you think I'm a Scrooge?"

Hope chuckled. "I never said that."

"You didn't have to. It was thoroughly implied." His tone was light and teasing as he held her close and began to hum along with the music.

"You certainly have your Scrooge moments but they're getting fewer and fewer."

"And that's a good thing?" he asked.

She nodded. "It's a great thing."

And then they danced together under the moonlight.

≈❧❧≈

Later, as they lay in Beckett's massive bed huddled under the blankets, Hope shivered.

"You're still cold?" Beckett asked and pulled her close.

"I know. Crazy, right?"

"I thought between the fire, the blankets…and me," he teased, "you'd certainly be warm by now, if not hot."

"Well, what we just did was pretty hot," she said and kissed his chest, "but I still feel a little cold."

He ran his hands up and down her back and smiled as she purred and pressed closer to him. It felt so good to hold her, to touch her and knowing how she was leaving in the morning was torturing him more than he thought possible. Beckett had gotten used to being alone. He didn't particularly like it, but he'd certainly gotten used to it and found there was less of a chance of getting hurt that way. But now, after meeting Hope and spending time with her, he found he had missed having someone with him, someone to talk to, someone to laugh with.

Suddenly, his hands stopped moving. "Don't go," he said quietly.

Hope lifted her head slightly and looked up at him. "I wasn't planning on going back to my room tonight."

He shook his head. "No. I mean tomorrow. Don't go. Stay and spend Christmas here with me."

Her eyes went a little wide. "I…I thought you didn't do Christmas?"

"I don't. Or rather, I haven't in a really long time. But I'd like to this year…with you."

The smile that crossed her face was almost as

bright as all the twinkly lights out on the property. "Really?" she asked with awe and wonder. "You really want to spend Christmas with me?"

Beckett nodded. "I know it's short notice and you have your brother to think about…"

She waved off the comment. "After what he did to me, it wasn't a high priority to spend Christmas with him. Besides, the way things turned out, I'm sure he'd rather spend the day with Merry and her family. And if her mother cooks anything like Merry, I won't mind missing that Christmas dinner." They both laughed.

"I can promise you that Norma will make a fabulous, five-star worthy meal for you."

"For us," Hope said, her expression suddenly serious.

"What?" he whispered. "What's the matter?"

It took a minute for Hope to collect her thoughts. "I still can't believe I'm here with you. I never thought I'd ever be here with G.B…"

Placing a finger over her lips to silence her, Beckett smiled weakly. "You have no idea how much I hate that name and the look it puts on your face when you say it. I can't change the things I've done to make you feel the way you do about me, Hope. I can only try to show you that it's not who I really am."

"But…earlier…on the phone…"

"I'm not going to lie to you, sometimes I have to be that guy when I'm doing business; otherwise people slack off and don't take you seriously. Maybe I've gotten too hard and too rigid over the years, I don't know. What I do know is that when we're together, I don't want to be that guy. You've made me remember how to relax and actually do something other than work."

She smiled at him. "You're a really nice guy when you're not working."

He slapped a hand over his heart and pretended to faint. "That almost sounded like a compliment."

"Oh!" she smacked his hand away playfully. "Are you fishing for compliments, G.B.?" she teased.

In the blink of an eye, he reversed their positions until she was pinned under him. "Maybe I am."

Hope stared up at him and a knowing smile crossed her lips. "I love spending time with you, Beckett. You make me feel very special."

"You are special," he said thickly. "You've turned my world upside down and I love every minute of it." He was trying not to analyze the fact that they had each used the word love. It wasn't a coincidence; it couldn't be. The reality was that he *was* falling in love with Hope and if he was reading her correctly, the feeling was mutual.

Reaching up, Hope cupped her hand at his nape and gently nudged him closer. "So you want me to stay?" she whispered.

Beckett nodded, emotion clogging his throat. "Always," he said before claiming her lips with his.

In the wee hours of the morning, Hope texted Ted and told him not to come and get her and that she'd explain later. Beckett had looked extremely pleased when she finished and shut the phone off.

They made plans to decorate the house and he promised they'd go into town the next day and do some shopping. She was looking forward to it. Actually, for the first time in months, Hope was actually looking forward to Christmas. And it was all thanks to the one man who had originally ruined it for her.

What an odd turn of events, she thought as she lay in his arms. It was as if she had gotten her very own Christmas wish and it was better than she ever imagined it could be. She wasn't foolish enough to believe this state of bliss was going to last forever. After all, they were safely cocooned away from the realities of life. Beckett may still be working, but it was nothing compared to what he did on a normal basis.

And then there was her brother.

Hope had no idea how they were going to deal with that whole situation. Right now, all thoughts of killing him were nixed because had he not left her stranded with Beckett, they wouldn't be here like this right now. Unfortunately, his stranding her here was the reason he was now out of a job. But no matter how bad she felt about it, she wasn't going to intercede on his behalf to get his job back. She told Beckett earlier that his business was none of hers and she meant it.

She just prayed it wasn't something that was going to come between them.

Chapter *Eight*

For the next three days, Hope felt like she was living in either a fairytale or a Hallmark Christmas movie; she couldn't decide. She and Beckett spent days decorating the lodge from top to bottom with all new Christmas decorations. That hadn't originally been the plan, but when they took the old ones out of storage they were definitely showing signs of age and rather than try to piece things together, he had declared since this was a fresh start, they deserved fresh decorations.

And the nights were beyond her wildest fantasies. For a man who had once seemed so selfish and self-centered, he more than changed that persona once they were alone. Hope was normally a woman who enjoyed a good night's sleep but when she was with Beckett, it didn't seem to matter. He made her feel sexy, wanted, cherished. And if that was the price to pay for feeling a little sleepy during the day, then she'd gladly deal with it.

Plus, it was a great excuse for an afternoon nap.

They had gone into town and practically bought out the entire holiday department of the local Target. While Beckett had loaded packages in the car, Hope ran to Starbucks to get them hot chocolates. They drank them while they drove through town deciding they'd cut their own tree down from the property around the lodge. Hope had been giddy at the idea. Her parents always had an artificial tree and because she lived alone, she had a small one herself. The thought of not only having a live tree, but cutting it down themselves, was almost too perfect.

While they handled those things, Norma had begun to bake and cook to prepare the Christmas feast. Hope thought it was a little soon to begin making a meal that was only going to be for the three of them, but decided to not say anything. Everyone was so happy that it would have been a sin to break the spell.

Which was why she chose to not answer any of her brother's calls. She did text him that she was fine and had a change of plans and she'd talk to him on Christmas Eve. Clearly he must have been relieved because he didn't push her for a further explanation, not that she knew how to explain the change in circumstances; she still couldn't believe them herself.

Something had definitely changed after their night dancing in the gazebo. Beckett was more affectionate with her and even though he still took several hours a day to work, he seemed way more at ease and relaxed. There was a spring in his step and he was always quick with a smile. Hope liked to think that she was responsible for it, but she had a feeling she was only part of it. Maybe Beckett was finally finding peace within himself. The thought made her smile.

"You've worked miracles here," Norma said Christmas Eve morning. Beckett had gone out to cut more wood for the fireplaces and it was just the two of them sitting at the kitchen table.

Hope shook her head. "It was a group effort."

"I'm not talking about the decorations. I'm talking about Beckett. I never thought I'd see the day when he willingly wanted to celebrate the holidays again. It's been so long." She paused and Hope saw tears well up in her eyes. "This house used to be filled to the rafters with people at Christmas. I've missed that–the laughter, the joy, the chaos. I pray someday he'll come to peace with his brother and sister and then we can have Christmas like we used to."

"Do you think…," Hope began and then paused. "Do you think he'd be open to having them here this year? Maybe you could call them?"

Norma's eyes went wide. "Oh, I don't think I could do that."

"Why not?"

She shook her head and took a sip of her tea. "It's not my place, Hope. Beckett's a very private person and he has his reasons for the way things are with his siblings. And as much as I'd like to point the finger at any one of them, it was all of their faults what happened."

"What did happen? Why doesn't he speak to them?"

A soft sigh came out as Norma placed her teacup on the table. Her expression was sad as she relayed the story of what had happened between Beckett and his siblings.

"So it wasn't jealousy that caused the rift." It wasn't a question, Hope just was trying to put the pieces together.

"No. But once Beckett's father passed, all of a sudden there were Logan and Julie trying to call in favors and get a place in the company–with Beckett's financing! They didn't want to earn a place or contribute anything; they wanted a piece of the pie without working for it, to just sit back and collect their money. His sister Julie was the one who broke his heart the most. She wasn't even asking on her own behalf. She wanted Beckett to financially back her boyfriend, well, Colton's her husband now, but back then he was just her boyfriend." She shook her head. "Beckett cut them both out of his life and what surprised me the most was how neither of them ever tried to see his side or call to apologize. Beckett's stubborn but I think he was genuinely hurt by their actions."

"And rightfully so. That's horrible." No more horrible than Ted leaving her behind to do his job so he wouldn't get fired, so she totally understood where Beckett was coming from. However, she wasn't sure she could completely cut her brother out of her life. She might be temporarily angry with him, but to never talk to him again? She just couldn't imagine it. "Do you think they'll ever make up?"

"It's been a long time. If it hasn't happened by now, I don't think it will."

"Maybe they all just need a little…nudge."

"That may be, but it's not going to be from me," Norma said as she shook her head again. "Those three are like my own children and I still talk to Logan and Julie all the time. I miss them terribly but I wouldn't betray Beckett by inviting them here without his permission."

"Do they ever talk about it?"

Norma nodded. "They've both admitted they handled things wrong but they feel Beckett overreacted too and that he's the one unwilling to open the lines of communication."

"Maybe I could mention it to him. You know, sort of feel him out."

Norma looked at her warily. "If anyone might be able to do it, it would be you. Just be prepared for Beckett not to be very open to the idea."

Hope chuckled. "Believe me, after this last week, I'm prepared for just about anything."

The Christmas tree looked spectacular.

The house was positively festive.

And Hope felt like she was going to throw up.

Alone in her room, she relished the quiet. Beckett had mentioned having a few more calls to make and even though it was Christmas Eve, Hope had no doubt he didn't have a problem wrapping up business when most people were getting ready to celebrate with their families.

She didn't mind. It gave her some time to get her thoughts together. She looked at her reflection in the mirror and smiled. It wasn't often that she dressed up; working from home by herself left very little reason to, but standing here now, she realized that she liked it.

The dress came down almost to her ankles but the entire garment hugged her body. In crushed hunter green velvet, she felt festive and pretty. The sleeves were long and she found herself pushing them up out of habit, but the look still worked. She kept her hair long and loose and even slipped on a pair of stilettos that matched the dress. Hope had no idea how dressed up Beckett was going to be but she figured this dress would work either way.

Norma had prepared a lovely meal but she had left an hour ago to spend the night with her own family. Hope knew how to get everything plated and served for just the two of them. That wasn't a problem. She was nervous, however, about bringing up the subject of his family. As much as she felt it was important and something they needed to discuss, she was so looking forward to the night that she didn't want to do anything to ruin it.

Her only hope was to play it by ear and see if there was a way to weave it into the conversation.

She was just about to step out of her room when her phone rang. Looking at the screen, she saw Ted's name pop up. "Merry Christmas," she said cheerily.

"What in the world is going on?" he demanded. "You haven't answered any of my calls and…"

"I texted you. Everything's fine. I just decided to stay and have Christmas here."

"With Mr. James?"

"With Beckett," she said and smiled at the fact how for five years her brother never bothered to find out Beckett's name.

"I don't understand, Hope. You freaked out about my leaving you there and then you decide not only to stay but to stay for Christmas. It doesn't make any sense. You guilted me about spending the holiday together and then you don't come home!"

"I know, I know," she said as she looked at her reflection and fluffed her hair. "It's hard to explain."

"Try me."

She told Ted about the time she had spent with Beckett, without knowing he was Ted's boss, before coming to the mountains. "I was shocked when I realized who he really was, and now that I've spent some time with him, I realized he's not so bad."

"He fired me, Hope! Or have you forgotten that?"

"No, I haven't forgotten, but you did that to yourself. There's nothing I can do about it."

"Sure you can! You can talk to him and convince him to give me my job back! The whole situation just got out of hand. Certainly now that you've spent so much time cozying up to him he'll listen to you."

"First of all, stop it. Second of all, I'm not cozying up to him for you or for anyone else. I like Beckett, a lot. And I'm not going to use the relationship we have for your benefit. If you want your job back, then you're going to have to come and talk to him–man to man."

"Geez, you're something else, you know that?" he snapped. "I can't believe after all the complaining you've done over the years about him, now you're…you're…what? You're dating him or something?"

"I jumped to the wrong conclusion." Sort of. "I needed to get to know him."

"Well I did know him, damn it! I knew him as my boss and you nagged the crap out of me about him! And now I'm screwed and out of a job and you're playing house with him!"

"No one's playing house and you're overreacting," she said calmly. "Look, we'll talk about this after I get home."

"I'm coming up there tomorrow," Ted said emphatically. "You need to come home and I know I should have done it sooner, but I'm driving up there first thing in the morning."

"No, you're not. Tomorrow is Christmas Day and we have plans."

"Then set another plate at the table because I'm going to be there."

"Ted…" But it was too late. He'd hung up. Hope knew it wasn't ideal, but the situation was only one of the elephants in the room and maybe the sooner they dealt with it the better. Plus, it was the exact opening she needed to introduce the subject of Beckett's siblings.

With a sigh, she opened the bedroom door and made her way down the stairs to the kitchen. "*Fa-*

la-la-la-la, la-la-la-la," she sang as she went. The dining room table was already set and a quick glance at the clock told her their appetizers would be ready to serve in less than ten minutes. There was no sign of Beckett yet, so she walked down to his office to see if he was still working.

He wasn't.

She walked into the study to see if he was in there and the sight of the tree all lit up just stopped her in her tracks and made her smile. "We did that," she whispered and reached out to touch one of crystal ornaments.

"Yes, we did," Beckett said from behind her.

Hope didn't turn around; she knew he'd come in close and wrap his arms around her. It was a habit he had and one she really loved. "I think it's the most beautiful tree in the world."

He chuckled. "I don't know about that, but it's certainly the most beautiful tree I've ever seen." He kissed her cheek. "And you're the most beautiful woman."

She blushed. No one had ever called her beautiful before, only Beckett. She turned in his arms and, thanks to her heels, she was the perfect height to kiss him properly without having to stretch. "Thank you," she whispered.

"I have to admit, I wasn't so sure how I'd feel about all of this, having the house decorated and actually celebrating, but with you here, it just feels…right."

No words could have meant more to Hope. She had felt the same way. This was different from any other Christmas she had ever celebrated and on some level she was expecting it to feel foreign or uncomfortable but everything about it just seemed to fit. It gave her hope that she was healing. She'd never get over missing her parents, but seeing how she wasn't alone and had something to look forward to was a wonderful feeling.

It would have been so easy to just stay like that, but the kitchen timer went off. "That would be our appetizers," Hope said and disengaged from Beckett's embrace and walked toward the kitchen.

"Can I help you with anything?"

"Why don't you pour us some wine while I make our plates?" Together they worked in silence and when they were ready to sit down, Beckett held out the chair for her before taking his own seat.

Holding up his glass, Beckett looked over at her and smiled serenely. "Shall we toast?" he asked and Hope nodded. "To a most surprising Christmas."

With her glass in hand, Hope reached out and touched hers to Beckett's. "To us."

The smile on Beckett's face broadened. "To us."

They drank and then began tasting the delicious hors d'oeuvres Norma had prepared for them. Each plate had a crab and risotto cake, two stuffed mushrooms, zucchini fritters and grilled scallops wrapped in bacon. After her first taste of the crab cake, Hope purred with delight. "Oh, my goodness. How does she do it?"

"She's amazing, right?" Beckett said as he popped a scallop into his mouth.

"I know she was making enough to take to her

family and was kind enough to leave these for us, but I'm so glad she did!"

After they were finished, they sat and talked about everything and nothing before it was time for the main course. "Is it wrong to say I'm still kind of full from the appetizers?" Hope asked as she stood when the second timer went off.

Beckett followed her into the kitchen with the dirty dishes. "No, it's not. Norma outdid herself this year. We can always keep the dinner warm and have it later if you'd like."

She considered her options and decided it would be a shame to reheat the crown roast. "Let's eat it now. We don't have to have a whole lot. Besides, once we're done eating, I have other plans for us." She winked at Beckett and almost laughed at the stunned expression on his face.

"What kind of plans?"

"I guess you'll just have to wait and see."

They worked together once again to put dinner on the table, neither speaking much. Hope knew she was rushing through the meal and she had a sneaking suspicion Beckett was doing the same. It was almost a relief when they each put their utensils down and declared themselves finished.

Hope cleared the table while Beckett did the dishes and when there was nothing left to do, he shut off the lights in the kitchen and came to stand in front of her. "I believe you mentioned something about plans for after dinner?" he teased.

"Did I?"

He nodded. "I believe you did."

Taking Beckett by the hand, she led him to the

study. There was a fire roaring in the fireplace and between it and the lights on the Christmas tree, there wasn't a need for any more. Hope walked over and flipped the wall switch to shut off all the excess lighting. Then she moved over to the tree and knelt down in front of it and motioned for Beckett to join her.

Silently, he sat beside her. Hope rested her head on his shoulder and sighed. "I know we didn't talk about it, but…I got you something."

He shifted and looked at her with something akin to shock. "Like a present?"

She nodded. "I don't expect anything in return," she said quickly. "I just wanted to give something to you. It's nothing big. I…you made me look forward to Christmas when I didn't think anything could and I want to thank you."

Hope reached under the tree and pulled out a medium-sized wrapped package and handed it to him. Much like he had on that first night when she gave him the tin of cookies, he didn't take it right away. "Please, Beckett."

He finally took it and Hope could tell he wasn't fully comfortable with the situation. Slowly, he began to unwrap it and once the paper was dispersed with, he looked up at her. "You really didn't have to do anything, Hope. We never talked about…"

"Christmas is about giving, not receiving. I wanted to give you something. It's nothing big. I mean, we went shopping together so I really didn't have a chance to look around too much. I hope you like this."

Beckett swallowed hard and opened the box. Inside was…a drawing. No…it was a sketchpad full of drawings. Looking up at her, he frowned. "I don't understand."

"Remember when I told you I used to draw comic books?"

He nodded.

"Well, while you've been working these last couple of days, I've been drawing this for you. It's silly, I know, but…it's the story of a man who is all alone in the world and then he discovers that he has superpowers. He creates beautiful places for people to stay and helps those who are also alone to celebrate the holiday that is most important to them."

Beckett watched her intently as she spoke, not looking at the book. "Does he have a cape?"

Hope visibly relaxed and smiled. "Of course. Every superhero should have a cape. No matter what they said in *The Incredibles*."

"I…I don't know what to say. This…this is the most amazing gift anyone has ever given me."

Her smile grew. "Good. I didn't know what to get the man who has everything."

"What if I'd already had a personalized, hand-drawn comic book? What would you have done then?" he teased.

Hope stood and took a step back. Reaching behind her, she tugged the zipper on her dress down and then shimmied a bit until it hung from her shoulders and then let it fall to the ground to pool at her feet.

"I must have been a very good boy this year,"

Beckett murmured reverently. Hope stood bathed in firelight and the glow of the lights on the tree wearing red silk and lace underwear, her stilettos and nothing else.

"I believe you have," she whispered.

Slowly, Beckett came to his feet, his hands shaking as he reached out to touch her. "You should have told me you were going to do this. I would have loved to unwrap you." His voice was thick and husky as his eyes devoured her.

"I left the most important pieces for you to handle," she said as she boldly stepped forward and pressed up against him from chest to toe. "Unwrap me, Beckett."

"My pleasure."

୶୶ଡ଼

Later, they were still on the floor of the study in front of the fire, but Beckett had found a blanket to cover them with. Hope's back was against his chest and she was using his arm as a pillow. He wished they had moved into his bedroom, but it seemed absolutely perfect for them to make love here in front of the tree, in front of the fire.

"Are you awake?" he asked softly and smiled when she barely nodded. "Because if you are, I actually have a present for you."

Slowly, Hope turned in his arms until she was facing him. "Oh, really?" she asked and then yawned. "Why didn't you say so earlier?"

"Because your gift blew me away. I was barely able to speak."

She giggled. "That was what I was going for."

"You know, a less secure guy might take that to mean you don't want them to talk."

Hope rolled her eyes. "Really? We're going to go there now?"

"You're right. Sorry."

"So…a present?"

"You're not the only one who had to be secretive," he said as he rolled her onto her back so that he could reach beyond her and pull a box out from under the tree. It was a bit larger than the one she had given him and square. Sitting up, he handed it to her.

Hope pulled the blanket up to cover herself a bit and took the gift from him. "Oh my goodness. It's heavy," she said as she smiled and looked at him. "What in the world…?"

"Just open it."

Delicately, she tore away at the tape and then did her best to take the wrapping paper off without actually ripping it. When she finished, she took the lid off of the box, moved the tissue paper aside and gasped. "Oh, Beckett…what…? Oh, it's beautiful!" Carefully, she pulled the musical snow globe from the box. The scene showed a house that looked a lot like Beckett's surrounded by trees and snow and when you shook the globe, it looked a lot like his did during the snowstorm. "What does it play?" she asked, her eyes never leaving the snowy scene.

"Wind it up and find out," he said, his voice gruff.

She did and when it began to play, tears welled

in her eyes. "Winter Wonderland" filled the room. "It's the most perfect gift I've ever received. Thank you." Leaning forward, she kissed him softly on the lips.

"No matter where you are, you'll always remember our Christmas here."

Hope swiped away some of the tears that now fell. "I won't need a snow globe to remind me. I'll always hold the memory dear, right here." Taking one of his hands in hers, she held it over her heart.

They sat like that until the music stopped and then Hope cuddled up beside him. "There are still quite a few presents under the tree," she said. "I know a few of them are the ones I had with me to bring to Tara and I did buy something for Norma and there's even one for Ted."

"Any more of them for me?" he asked, sounding a little like a kid.

"Maybe. But you'll have to wait until tomorrow to open them."

He pulled back and looked at her. "I was only kidding, Hope. Please tell me you didn't do anything else."

"I know how many gifts I put under that tree. What about you? Who are all those other gifts for?"

He shrugged. "There are a few there for Norma and I know she put a couple under there for both me and you."

"Oh, she didn't," Hope said, feeling humbled that Norma would even think of doing something like that for her.

"She's a good person."

Hope nodded in agreement. "What time will

195

she be back tomorrow?"

"That depends. I told her not to rush back so it probably won't be until tomorrow night. Why?"

She sighed. "I think Ted's coming in the morning. I told him not to, but he's freaked out because I'm still here and that I've asked him not to come. I didn't want him to ruin anything, especially not our Christmas, but I can't guarantee he won't show up here and make a scene."

Beckett knew it was a possibility. Reality was bound to intrude sooner or later. It just sucked that it was sooner. "We knew he was going to come back eventually," he finally said. "I guess we'll have to deal with that tomorrow."

"That's it? You don't have anything else to say about it?"

"Hope, he's your brother. Your family. I'll admit it makes things a little awkward, all things considered, but we'll handle it. Right?" He skimmed a hand down her cheek and rested his forehead against hers.

It would have been the perfect time to mention his family, but Hope just didn't have it in her. Their time was already being cut short thanks to Ted, so she didn't want to waste any time arguing with Beckett unnecessarily.

As if reading her mind, Beckett stood and held out a hand to her. "What do you say we move this to someplace that's a little more comfortable than the floor?"

"That could be just about anywhere," she said saucily as she rose to her feet. "But I'm hoping you mean your bed." Then she let out a screech as

Beckett scooped her up into his arms and started to make his way across the room. "Beckett!"

"You're not the only one who had plans tonight," he said and kicked the bedroom door closed behind him.

&ᴠꙮ&

"Okay, I know how I was able to get your gifts without you seeing them, but how did you happen to manage all of this?" Beckett asked the next morning. They were back on the floor in front of the Christmas tree opening gifts. He had already opened a scarf and a sweater from Hope and she was handing him another box.

"I have a feeling we shared a personal shopper," she said with an impish grin and took a sip of her hot chocolate. "Norma offered to pick up whatever I needed when she went shopping the other day. I gave her my list and she got just about everything I asked for."

He laughed. "I did the same thing." He shook his head. "The poor woman. She probably just needed to get one or two things from the store and we had her doing all of our shopping for us!"

Hope couldn't help but join in on the laughter. "I don't think she minded. This whole situation seemed to amuse her."

"I don't doubt it for a minute," he said and tore into his gift. "Oh my God! I wanted to get this game but I haven't had the time to order it!" He flipped the video game case over in his hands and read the description. "I've heard a lot of great things about it. The reviews are all raving about it."

"You were missing quite a few of the top games so I was hoping you'd like this one. We may have to set it up after breakfast and play it. I've only had the chance to play it once or twice so there won't be an unfair advantage."

"Ha, ha. You you're hilarious. We'll see if you can beat me a second time."

"Sure. Let's see how long you can pay attention this time," she teased.

Without a word, Beckett reached under the tree and pulled out a box and handed it to Hope. "I'm afraid this is one category where I kind of floundered. I don't know exactly what you like so…I hope you like it."

Hope didn't doubt that she would. She tore open the wrapping and tossed it aside. Taking the lid off the top, she smiled. Inside was a beautiful cashmere scarf with a matching hat and gloves. She ran her hands over them and loved the way they felt. "They're beautiful! Thank you!"

Beckett loved the look of pure delight on Hope's face. If he had purchased anything this simple for some of the women he'd dated in the past, they would have been annoyed with him. But not Hope. It just proved to him yet again that she was an incredible woman, one who was with him for him and not his money.

"I love you," he said before he could stop himself.

Hope dropped the gift, her eyes wide. "What?"

Beckett smiled and reached for her, caressing her face, cupping her cheek. "I love you." This wasn't how he'd planned it. Hell, he hadn't planned it at all. But if he had, Beckett knew he would have staged the scene for something a little more romantic than the two of them sitting on the floor on Christmas morning in their robes. He would have had champagne and flowers and they'd be dancing slowly by the fire or something equally...

"I love you too." Those wide eyes softened as she pressed a hand to his. And then they closed as Beckett leaned forward and kissed her, slowly and thoroughly. They sank down onto the carpet, his hands never leaving her face, her hand never leaving his.

When he finally pulled back, he looked at Hope in amazement. "How did we get here?"

She shook her head. "I don't know. It doesn't seem possible. It all happened so fast."

"It doesn't make it any less real, Hope. I love you."

"That's the best Christmas present you could ever give me," she said as a tear rolled down her cheek.

Slowly, they sat back up. "I guess I don't have to give you this last present then," Beckett said lightly and went to stand up.

"Oh no you don't," she chuckled. "I get to open that or no breakfast for you."

He pretended to contemplate his options before kissing her soundly and handing her the gift. "I really took a gamble on this one," he began nervously. "Norma didn't help me with it. It's just something," he stopped and paused. "It's something I wanted you to have."

Hope looked over at him with love in her eyes. "I already have everything I could ever want," she said simply. "Whatever is in this box is just a bonus."

Beckett wasn't so sure and he felt his whole body go tense as he watched her open the gift. Then he watched the confusion on Hope's face as she lifted the folder from the box.

"I…I don't understand. What is this?"

"It's a contract," he said slowly.

Her brow furrowed. "A contract? For what?"

"A year ago, you submitted a business plan to me for a café to go in one of my hotels. I rejected it based on the fact that you were related to one of my employees. Your plan was solid, Hope, and I shouldn't have just disregarded it based on a hang up I have. That contract states that you have the option to open your café in any one of the hotels in the chain. Not just in Raleigh, not just in North Carolina even, but any hotel in the chain, in the world."

When Hope didn't say anything, Beckett went on to explain it a bit further. "James Enterprises will build to your specifications and supply all of the appliances and furniture you need as well as your startup inventory."

Her eyes went wide again. "Beckett? Are you serious?" she asked and he nodded. "No. It's…it's too much. I didn't…I mean, I never…" She placed the folder down and stood up and began to pace. "I can't accept it." She crossed her arms protectively across her middle.

Beckett quickly stood and placed his hands on her shoulders. "Hey, what's this all about? I thought this would make you happy?"

She quickly stepped out of his grasp. "No. It's not right. I can't ask you to do that. Any of it."

"But you didn't ask, Hope. I offered. It's a gift."

She shook her head vehemently. "Don't you see, by accepting that, I'm no better than all of those people you hate. The people who you say take advantage of you. I'd be one of them!"

"No! No you wouldn't. You could never be like that, Hope. I know that." He reached for her again and forced her to look at him. "What is this all about?"

Tears welled up in her eyes. "Your family," she said sadly. "Norma told me about Logan and Julie and the things they asked of you. It was wrong of them, I know that, and you were right to be offended by the things they expected of you, but by accepting this gift, I'm no better than they are."

"Hope, you are nothing like them!" he said as his voice rose with frustration. "Don't compare yourself to them. You're better than that! Better than them!"

"How can you say that? They're your family!"

Now it was his turn to step away. "Don't you think I know that? Don't you think that is the exact reason why it hurt so much more? All at once, it seemed like they stopped seeing me as their brother and started seeing me as a way to make some easy money! I worked hard my entire life to get where I am now! I may have inherited the company, but it doesn't mean I didn't give everything I had to it before then! And then they just…"

"I know, Beckett, I know," she said softly, trying to soothe him. "When your family betrays you or you feel like they've betrayed you, it's the worst kind of hurt."

"I can never forgive them for that. I'm here, I'm alone because they felt if I wouldn't finance them, then I wasn't worth knowing."

That one statement broke her heart. "Beckett, have you ever tried to talk to them about it? Have you talked to either of them since it happened?"

He shook his head. "No."

"You need to. You need to clear the air. I'm sure if they knew how…"

"It doesn't matter," he interrupted roughly. "I don't want to discuss it. It's done and over with and what I've drawn up for you is about me giving you something. You didn't come here and sleep with me in order to gain some real estate. I know that. You're not that kind of person."

"I'm glad you realize that," she said with a nervous laugh.

Beckett stared at her hard. "I knew from the moment I met you that you were different. It had nothing to do with the fact that you didn't like me. You are someone with morals and a kind heart. On so many levels, you're too good for me, but damn it, that didn't stop me from wanting you…from falling in love with you."

"I don't want this between us, Beckett. I can't accept this gift. I wouldn't feel right about it. The café? It's a dream of mine I've always had, but it's a dream I want to accomplish on my own. I need to prove to myself that I can do it. If you do it for me, it's just not going to be the same."

"Hope…"

She reached out and gently touched his face. "You have no idea how much it means to me that you even wanted to do it. No one's ever given me so much."

"Can we just…table it for now? Maybe, sometime in the future, you might consider it?"

She smiled sadly. "Okay. But I don't want you to get your hopes up and I don't want you to push me on this."

He nodded and then pulled her into his embrace. Together they stood like that in front of their tree until their emotions were more under control. "How about some breakfast?" he asked quietly.

"That sounds good to me. I asked Norma what she normally made on Christmas morning, but she left the decision up to me. I have a great recipe for gingerbread waffles. What do you think?"

After a light kiss to the tip of her nose, Beckett said, "I think anything you make is amazing."

"Aw, aren't you sweet?" They walked into the kitchen and began working together, but Hope still had something on her mind. "Beckett?"

"Hmm?"

"I know it's really none of my business but…"

"But…?"

"Maybe you should call your brother and sister. It's Christmas. You don't have to hash anything out. Just call them and say 'Hey, Merry

Christmas.'"

His expression hardened for a brief second. "I don't think so."

"They're the only family you have," she said pleadingly. "Don't you miss them?"

"I did for a while. Now I'm used to it. And what about you? What's going to happen when Ted gets here? Are you just going to run up and hug him and wish him a Merry Christmas? I thought you were on the verge of killing him."

"I'll admit I was really ticked off at him, but I couldn't imagine not having him in my life. It would destroy me. He's the only family I have. What he did benefited me–benefited us! Do you think we'd be here like this right now if it wasn't for Ted being such a jerk?"

Beckett couldn't help but laugh. "Probably not, but it still doesn't excuse what he did to you, Hope. He had no idea things would work out like this! He left you stranded and alone with a stranger!"

"You were hardly a stranger. He's worked for you for five years. In his mind, you could walk on water. He idolizes you!"

That stopped Beckett in his tracks. "What?"

"Oh, please. You can't tell me you didn't realize that. He would do anything you asked of him because he thinks the world of you. All he's ever wanted was for you to tell him he's done a good job or that you liked his ideas. He was killing himself to get you to notice him. So while he wasn't thinking anything romantic was going to happen here, Ted would have trusted you with his life. And mine."

That was a humbling thought. "Do you think I was too hard on him?" he asked, his voice low.

Hope nodded slowly. "I know and understand why you did what you did, Beckett. But maybe everything doesn't always have to be so black and white. People screw up. They make mistakes. And it's all right to get ticked off and yell and let them know they screwed up, but maybe you don't have to make them dead to you because of it."

He studied her for a long time while neither spoke. "Fine. I'll think about it. When he gets here, we'll sit and talk. I can't guarantee that I'm ready to give him his job back, but I promise to talk to him like a rational human being. Okay?"

"That's all I can ask for," she said sweetly and kissed his cheek before turning to start the waffles. As if she'd worked in this kitchen her entire life, Hope whipped up the waffle batter and got the coffee started. Beckett walked out of the kitchen to clean up their wrapping paper debris in the study before setting the dining room table for them.

Hope was just putting the last of the waffles on a platter when the doorbell rang. "Showtime," she whispered.

Beckett popped his head into the kitchen. "I think your brother's here. Want to come to the door with me so you can see how nice I can be?"

"Oh, stop. I know you can be nice and besides, I trust you to keep your word." Together they walked to the door and Beckett smiled at her before he opened it. "Hey, Ted!" she said with a big smile. "Merry…"

"You son of a bitch!" Ted snarled right before

he pulled back and punched Beckett right in the face.

Chapter *Nine*

"Oh my God!" Hope cried, but she wasn't exactly sure who she was addressing. "Ted! What in the world?"

To his credit, Beckett didn't swing back. He stumbled back a few feet but didn't fall. He rubbed his jaw where Ted had hit him, but kept his anger in check, while glaring at Ted.

Hope ushered her brother in and shut the door. "I cannot believe you just did that! How could you?"

"Are you kidding me?" Ted yelled. "This is the same man who commanded all of my time, fired me when my fiancée was injured and now you open the door and it's obvious that you're more than just a guest here…I mean, you're not defending him, are you?"

A loud sigh escaped before Hope could stop it. "Did it ever occur to you to maybe try to talk about it first?"

"I tried to talk. Last week if you'll recall. I did my best to try to get him to listen to me, but he wouldn't. And now, knowing all that you do, you're still here all cozied up to him! How could you, Hope?"

This was just the kind of discussion she had hoped to avoid. "Okay, let's just…calm down. I was just putting breakfast on the table. Why don't we all go and sit down, have something to eat, and discuss this calmly, okay?"

Neither man spoke as they followed her into the dining room. Once they were seated and Hope had made up their plates, she looked over at Beckett and touched his jaw. "I think you need some ice for that. I'll be right back." She heard Beckett try to stop her, but she needed a minute to herself and preparing an ice pack seemed like the perfect excuse.

"How is your fiancée?" Beckett asked calmly as the two men eyed one another across the table.

"She's doing better. She'll be on crutches for about six weeks and she's bruised all over. She was lucky; it could have been much worse."

Beckett nodded. "Are her parents still in town?"

"Yes. It only made sense for them to stay through the holidays. It made Merry feel better."

Beckett's lips twitched at the mention of her name, but he hid it behind his napkin. "I'm sure it does." He paused. "Listen, Ted, I realize I was a little irrational last week when Hope showed up here and…"

"Yes, you were. I've worked very hard for you and you wouldn't allow me a day to go and make sure my fiancée was all right. I've never lied to you in all the years I've worked for you. You should have trusted me."

"I know and…"

"Now, thanks to you, Hope is furious with me. She never gets mad at me. I mean, sometimes she gets annoyed, but she gets over it. But this whole situation? She wouldn't talk to me and when she did, it was to yell at me."

"You deserved it," Beckett said. "You abandoned her. You dumped her stuff in the snow and stole her car. She went out of her way to let you know about Merry and you thanked her by leaving her here with a guy she hated."

"Clearly she got over it," Ted mumbled.

"Yeah, she got over it, but it doesn't make what you did all right, Ted. She's going to forgive you. You're her brother and the only family she has. She loves you and she deserves to have someone in her life who has her back. It seems to me she does a lot of stuff for you and you don't reciprocate."

"How can I? I'm always working!"

Beckett knew he had a point.

"Although, I guess that will change now. I'm hopeful my next job won't demand so much of my time so I can actually have a life outside of the office."

"Listen, Ted, about that…"

Hope came back into the room. "Here's the ice." She looked at the two of them as she slowly sat down. "How are the waffles? Have you tried them yet?"

Beckett reached for the syrup and poured some on before cutting into his breakfast. "Mmm…delicious. Why am I not surprised?"

She beamed under his praise. "Ted, try them. They're the gingerbread waffles I told you I wanted to try." She waited until he took a bite before tasting her own. Silence was a good thing at the moment. There was no doubt Beckett and Ted had been talking while she was out of the room, but Hope had no idea what was said or if anything had been resolved.

And then the silence began to grate on her nerves. "So," she began brightly, "what did Merry get you for Christmas, Ted?"

He shrugged. "A sweater."

Figures. "And what did you get her?"

"A vacuum."

"And they say romance is dead," she said cheekily and smiled even bigger when Ted frowned at her. "Oh, come on. Don't be like that. It's Christmas."

He placed his utensils down–loudly. "I just don't understand what's going on here. A week ago, you hated him!" he yelled while pointing at Beckett. "You would freak out if I even mentioned his name! And now you're here playing house with him and…"

"To be fair, Ted," she interrupted, "I didn't choose to stay here. You left me here."

"So…what? You made the best of a bad situation by sleeping with him?"

"That's enough," Beckett said in a tone that left

no room for argument. "I don't like what you're implying at all. What happened between me and your sister is none of your business."

"Well I think it is," Ted said with a hint of confidence before turning toward Hope. "I'm sure everything is nice and everything is sweet right now, but it's going to change. Once you leave here, he's going to be the same guy who you hated. Do you think he's going to stop being a workaholic overnight for you? Do you think he's going to actually have any time for you?"

"Ted," she interrupted but her brother wouldn't be deterred.

"Right now he didn't have a choice because he was snowed in here with limited internet access and with little hope of getting people on the phone because normal companies close for the holidays. He was killing time with you, Hope. Trust me. In the five years I worked for him, no one's ever seen him leave the damn office. You mark my words, you continue this…this…whatever it is with him when you're back home and you'll end up alone."

It was as if Ted had reached into her head and pulled out her every insecurity regarding what would happen once she and Beckett left the lodge.

"Don't do this, Hope. Don't put your hopes and dreams into a man like him. He's not worth it. He'll break your heart and he won't even care."

"I'm sitting right here, damn it!" Beckett snapped.

Ted glared at him. "Yeah, I know. Go ahead and deny it," he dared. "Go ahead and tell Hope you're going to cut back on your hours and you're going to make her your top priority." He sat back and waited and then turned back to Hope. "He can't, Hope. He can't and he won't."

No words would come. It was as if her vocal cords were paralyzed. She and Beckett had been living a fantasy existence here but it wasn't real. None of it was real. Well, that wasn't completely true. She knew her feelings for Beckett were real. She knew she loved him. Unfortunately, she knew her brother was right and the fact that Beckett wasn't arguing or denying any of it spoke volumes.

As if to put the final nail in the coffin, Ted leaned forward and said, "Family isn't important to a guy like him, Hope. Look what he did to poor Jerome. He didn't care that my fiancée was hurt. He didn't care that he was keeping me here away from my family for Christmas…"

"You made that choice," Beckett said darkly.

"I only received two days off when mom and dad died. That was all the time I was given. If I took longer, my job would have been in jeopardy. Do you remember that?"

She nodded slowly, her heart beating frantically. "I do."

"Does he even have family? He was willing to work through the holidays so if he has them, he doesn't care enough about them to want to see them."

"Not all families are close, Ted," she defended quietly.

"I know family is important to you, Hope," he said and reached out and touched one of her hands. "Could you really be with someone who didn't feel the same way? Where does that leave you for the next holiday? Or on occasions that are important to you? If you stay with him, you're going to be alone for all of them."

"That's enough," she cried. "Stop it. Just stop it!" With a strangled sob, she got up and ran from the room.

❧

Beckett sat back at watched Hope flee the room.

Was this really how people saw him? Was Ted right? Worse, did Hope believe him? He was torn between going after her or staying here and hashing things out with Ted. He glared at the man who had essentially ruined everything.

"If you care at all about my sister, you'll end this," Ted said quietly. "You know I'm right. You're not going to stop working long hours and ignoring everyone else's feelings. She deserves better than that."

In his heart, Beckett wanted to believe he could be the kind of man who was everything Hope needed, but now he wasn't so sure. An hour ago he was confident that he could, but after listening to Ted, his confidence was slightly shattered.

"Let her go," Ted said, all the anger and animosity of moments ago gone. "She's had a hard enough time of it since our parents died. She needs someone who is going to be there for her, someone who is going to put her first. We both know that's not you."

Hope came back into the room and came to stand beside Beckett. It was obvious she had been crying. "I think you should go, Ted," she said quietly. "I'm sorry you drove all this way, but under the circumstances, it would be better for you to leave."

Beckett watched the sadness on Hope's face and knew he was to blame. Because of the way he was, because of the person he was, she was arguing with the only family she had. He had done this. And now he had to make it right.

"Actually," he said, his voice gruff, "I think you should both leave."

"What?" she cried.

Standing, Beckett put a little distance between the two of them. "Your brother's right, Hope. Once I get back to the office, nothing's going to change. I have a major corporation to run and I can't just drop everything so we can hang out."

"Hang out?" she parroted. "That's not what we've been doing, that's not what…"

"Look, I guess I got all caught up in what was going on here. I couldn't work, you couldn't leave, I mean…it was a fun way to spend the time." He hated every word coming out of his mouth and hated even more the devastation they were putting on Hope's face. "You were a nice diversion."

"Why are you saying this? Why are you doing this?" she cried. "An hour ago you told me you loved me!"

He shrugged, unable to look at her. "I was caught up in the moment, I guess." And he knew in that moment he had done it. He had lost her.

214

"Bastard," she whispered.

"I never pretended to be anything else. You just saw what you wanted to see."

Hope stared at him as tears streamed down her face. "Go to hell, Beckett."

And there was the thing.

He was already there.

❦

The drive home was spent in silence. Several times Ted tried to talk to her, but Hope spent the entire drive looking out the window and watching the miles take her farther and farther away from Beckett.

They had been happy. At least, she'd been. How could she have been so wrong, so hopelessly wrong? Was Beckett right? Had she only been seeing what she wanted to see? No. He took her dancing in the snow. He had decorated his house for Christmas for her. But why? If he truly didn't love her and didn't see or want a future with her, why do all of those things?

There was never going to be an answer because she was never going to see him again. With Ted no longer working for James Enterprises, there was no excuse to run into him anywhere. It's not like their paths had crossed much before.

The thought of never seeing Beckett was almost more than Hope could bear. Her chest ached and she let out a shaky breath.

"Are you all right?" Ted asked softly, but she ignored him.

When they arrived back at her house, Ted helped her carry her things in, including the gifts Beckett had gotten for her for Christmas, but she didn't ask him to stay. Once she was inside, she put down her suitcase and her purse, walked straight through to her bedroom and shut the door. Ted must have taken the hint because not long after, she heard the front door close.

And then finally–*finally!*–she allowed herself to cry. It was the kind of soul-searing, gut-wrenching cry she hadn't allowed herself to have while still at Beckett's house, the kind of cry she hadn't had since her parents died.

Curled up in her bed, with all the lights out, Hope focused on just being able to breathe. In and out. In and out.

And realized that now she was well and truly all alone in the world.

A week later she was still feeling that way. Ted had called her several times a day but she never answered. Even Merry had called a time or two but she ignored those calls as well.

It was New Year's Eve and her plans consisted of sitting on the couch in her yoga pants and an oversized t-shirt eating ice cream and leftover Christmas cookies while watching old movies. Maybe she'd stay awake until midnight but she doubted it.

A noise by the front door had Hope nearly jumping out of her skin. Turning around, she found

Ted standing in the doorway. "That's not what the emergency key is for," she snapped and sat back down on the couch.

"What are you doing? Why aren't you ready?" he asked as he strolled into the room and helped himself to a cookie.

Hope looked at him as if he'd lost his mind. "What are you even talking about? Ready for what?"

He sighed loudly and sat down on the arm of the couch. "The Collins' party remember?"

"No."

He rolled his eyes. "I told you about it at Thanksgiving. You know Ally and Mike. They throw a big New Year's party every year. They're awesome. I asked you if you wanted to go and you said yes."

"Well now I'm saying no," she said and went back to reclining on the couch as she reached for a cookie.

"You can't say no now. It's too late. The party's tonight and it would be rude to not show up."

"So you go. Tell them I'm sick or something. I don't care." With the remote in her hand, she began to scan the channels for something to watch.

"Come on, take pity on me. Merry didn't want to go out because she's still sore and now I don't have a date for New Year's."

"Yeah? Join the club."

"Hope," he said with a smile as he nudged her with his elbow. "I'm unemployed and I'm dateless. It's been a crappy year. Can't we go and ring in the new one together and have some sort of hope for the future? Please?"

Ugh, she hated when he started making sense. "I'm not dressed to go anywhere, Ted. And I don't have anything to wear to a party. My wardrobe is seriously limited."

"Merry said you might use that excuse," he chuckled as he stood and walked back toward the front door.

Hope looked over her shoulder and saw him pick up a large shopping bag and bring it back to the couch. "What's this?"

"This, is a fabulous dress for you to wear tonight."

"Tell me you did not go shopping for a dress for me. That's just creepy."

"Actually, Merry and I were at the mall yesterday because she was getting a little stir-crazy sitting around the house. So we were strolling around, well, I was pushing her in a wheelchair because it was easier to get around and…"

"Ted!" she snapped. "Focus!"

"Oh, right. Anyway, we were in the dress department of some store and she saw this dress on the mannequin and said she thought it was the perfect dress for you. So we bought it."

Dread settled in the pit of her stomach. If Merry's taste in dresses was like her taste in food and everything else in her life, Hope was certain she would pull out something that would be considered conservative by the Amish.

Without reaching into the bag, she sat up and looked at her brother. "Look, it's not like I don't appreciate the effort, because I do. But I'm really not feeling very festive."

He sighed and sat down beside her and put his arm around her. "It's okay. I get it. Merry mentioned you might say that too. So she said to tell you that if you didn't want to go to the party, she'd have her parents bring her over here and she'll make dinner for all of us. Her lasagna is really quite good."

And there it was! The deciding factor!

"Fine. I'm going to take a shower and get dressed. Give me thirty minutes," she said with a huff and grabbed the bag from the sofa.

She didn't see the grin on Ted's face as she walked away.

❧

"I'm glad you had some leftover cookies. I hate showing up places empty-handed," Ted said as they drove off to the party.

"Yeah, because that's what most people bring for New Year's. Cookies." She snorted with disgust. "You could have picked up a bottle of champagne to bring. That's traditional."

"Oh, hush. Since when do we want to be traditional?"

"Um…Ted?" she asked when they turned onto a very familiar street. "What are we doing at your old office?"

"It's on the way and I have to turn in my security badge and stuff before tomorrow."

"And you waited until now to do it?" she cried.

"How could you do this to me? I don't want to be here! What if Beckett's here?"

"He's not," Ted said, parking the car. "I already called and checked. I have to hand in all of my security passes and work files before the end of the year. At least, that's what his Lordship said on the message he left me."

Hope slouched down in her seat just in case.

"Come on. Walk in with me. I don't want to do this alone. I feel like such a loser."

"Ted, I don't think…"

"Just do it," he whined and walked around and pulled her out of the car.

"Fine. But if we run into Beckett, I will definitely kill you."

"Great. Consider me warned," he teased and tugged her along behind him. He carried a box under one arm and smiled at her over his shoulder.

"I don't see what you're so happy about," she muttered. "You're officially ending your job here."

He shrugged. "I'm choosing to look at it as starting a new phase of my life."

Sure, whatever, she thought as they made their way to the door. Not wanting to even look at the building, Hope looked down at her feet as they approached the door.

"Good evening, Mr. Cooper. It's good to see you again, Sir."

Hope looked up and gasped with surprise. "Jerome! What are you doing here? I thought…I mean, I heard…"

"Tonight's my first night back on the job," he said with a bright smile. "Mr. James called me himself and gave me my job back along with an apology. Normally I'm here until midnight, but he said to leave at ten so I can ring in the New Year with my wife."

"Wow," she said quietly. "That's...that's wonderful. Really. I'm so happy for you."

Ted had walked away and placed a box on Jerome's desk by the door and pulled out a tin of cookies. He looked at Hope and winked. "You really don't think I'd only bring cookies to a party, do you?" He laughed. "I knew you had wanted Jerome to have some of these before Christmas, but I wanted to surprise you with seeing him for yourself."

Jerome took the tin from Ted and thanked him before turning back to Hope. "I'm telling you, it was like a Christmas miracle," he said. "My wife and I were trying to figure out where I was going to find work once the holidays were over and then the day after Christmas, Mr. James called me at home and apologized and asked if I wanted my old job back. With a raise!"

Emotions clogged Hope's throat so all she could do was nod.

"Anyway, the extra money will go a long way with helping with the medical bills. Although Mr. James said he's going to help me find a specialist to help Arlene with her asthma." He smiled. "I think Mr. James must have been visited by those three ghosts Dickens talked about in that Christmas story because he's like a different man."

"We really need to go," Ted said and clapped Jerome on the back. "Happy New Year, Jerome."

"You too, Mr. Cooper. And you too, Miss Cooper. Thank you for the cookies. Arlene and I will enjoy them tonight as we watch the ball drop." And then he walked over and hugged her.

Hope was nearly openly weeping by the time they were back at Ted's car.

"Why are you crying?" Ted asked gently as they climbed in. "I thought you'd be happy! I thought seeing how Jerome got his job back would perk you up."

"It did. It does. I'm just…I can't believe Beckett did that."

Ted didn't comment and instead pulled out of the parking lot and in the direction of the party. He knew Hope's mind was probably swirling with ideas as to why Beckett did what he did and he just wanted to let her have some time to absorb it all.

Fifteen minutes later, they pulled up in front of a large, three-story townhouse. Hope seemed to snap out of her trance and look around. "Wow. I didn't realize Ally and Mike lived in such a place."

"I guess business is booming," Ted said as he climbed from the car. He reached into the backseat and pulled out a bottle of champagne.

"I'm so glad you remembered some of the manners mom tried to teach you," Hope said with a chuckle as she closed the car door. Looking at her reflection in the car window, she had to admit that Merry didn't do a bad job with the dress. It was a classic little black dress–sleeveless and came to just above the knee and showed off her curves. Paired with her black stilettos and a red pashmina, Hope felt like she was looking pretty festive.

As if reading her mind, Ted came up beside her and kissed her cheek. "You look beautiful. Thank you for being my date tonight."

She hugged him and laughed. "What an exciting pair we are, sibling dates for a New Year's party. Let's make a pact right now to never do this again."

Ted laughed out loud and turned them toward the house. "Deal."

They rang the bell and waited. Hope shivered from the cold. "I probably should have worn a…" The words died in her throat as Beckett answered the door. She stared at him and then at Ted. "What…? I…I don't understand."

"Please come in," Beckett said with a serene smile. "I know it's cold out there tonight."

Hope's feet were frozen to the spot. With a little nudge, Ted got her to move and step up into the house. He smiled and shook hands with Beckett before moving into the house and greeting people. Hope still couldn't seem to make herself follow.

Beckett stepped in close and put his hands on her shoulders. "You're freezing," he said softly. "Please come inside and warm up."

She snapped out of her stupor and looked up at him. "No…no, I…I need to leave." Doing her best to move away from him, she found Beckett's hands held her in place. She sagged as her eyes filled with tears. "Why? Why are you here?"

He shrugged. "I live here."

Straightening slightly, she frowned. "But…Ted said Mike and Ally lived here. Why would he…?"

"Lie to you?"

Hope nodded.

"Because I asked him to. I knew you wouldn't come if I asked and if you knew you were coming to a party I was hosting, you wouldn't come. So we concocted a story that would get you to come out tonight."

And suddenly, she wasn't sad, she was angry. "Why? Are you bored? Looking for a way to pass the time? It's New Year's Eve, Beckett. I'm sure you could have gone to any number of parties and found a nice…*distraction*." She sneered the word and wanted to kick him for making her remember the horrible things he'd said.

His hands skimmed down her arms until his hands could clasp hers. "You were never just a distraction to me, Hope. I'm so sorry I said that. You're so much more to me."

"But…"

"I promise we'll talk about this, but there are some people I'd really like you to meet first."

"Beckett, I…I really don't want to meet anyone. I want to leave. Please. Maybe we can talk some other time. I…I just can't deal with this right now."

"Five minutes," he said quietly, resting his forehead against hers. "Just give me five minutes and if you still want to leave, I'll tell Ted to take you home. I promise."

Hope sighed and had to fight against the urge to lean her entire body against his. How was it possible that she was still so mad at him and yet so attracted to him at the same time? Oh, yeah. She was still in love with him.

Dammit.

"Fine. Five minutes," she said, but refused to meet his gaze. Hugging the pashmina close, she allowed Beckett to take her by the hand and lead her into the large living room where there were about a dozen people milling about. She spotted Ted immediately and saw him talking to…Merry. Merry? What in the world? There was an older couple standing beside them and Hope had to assume those were Merry's parents.

Great. Now she'd have an audience of future family members to witness her running out of here. Fabulous.

Beckett stopped and Hope pulled her eyes from her brother to see why they were stopping.

"Hope, this is Logan, my brother. Logan, this his Hope," Beckett said affectionately.

"It's a pleasure to meet you," Logan said. He was a younger version of Beckett but a little stockier. He took her hand in his and shook it. "I've heard a lot about you. I'm glad you were able to make it tonight."

"Thank you," she said and cursed the tremble in her voice.

"This is my fiancée Debbie," Logan said as a petite blonde came to stand beside him.

"It's nice to meet you," Debbie said with a big smile. She clung lovingly to Logan's side and Hope couldn't help but smile back.

"It's nice to meet you too," she finally said.

They didn't move but Hope noticed a few other people moving in their direction. Beckett tucked her close to his side, his arm around her waist. "Julie, Colton, I'd like you to meet Hope. Hope, this is my sister Julie and her husband."

"It's a pleasure to meet you," Hope said, shaking each of their hands. Julie had the same dark hair as Beckett and Logan and an easy-going smile. She was also very pregnant. Hope couldn't help but look at her belly and Julie chuckled.

"We've still got another month to go," she said and smiled as Colton stepped closer and rubbed his hand over her belly. "Colton keeps saying it's twins, but the doctors assure me there's only one in there."

"We'll see," Colton said with a wink.

"Oh, Hope! You're here!" Norma came over and quickly embraced her. "I was hoping you'd make it. I still have your Christmas present waiting for you. I put in under the tree over there so don't let me forget." She kissed Hope on the cheek. "And thank you for the lovely bath set. I love all of those salts and scrubs and lotions. It feels like I have my very own spa."

"You're very welcome. I'm glad you liked them," Hope said as she found herself relaxing. Ted walked over and handed her a glass of wine and kissed her on the cheek.

"When you get a minute, I'd love to introduce you to Merry's parents. They're very excited to meet you."

She nodded in agreement and continued to look around the room as conversation flowed around her. Beckett leaned in close, his lips against her ear. "Do you still want to leave?" he whispered.

"I...I don't know," she said honestly.

"Will you all excuse us for a few minutes?" Beckett asked the group and they all waved them off and smiled and went about their own discussions. Beckett led her from the room and up the stairs and didn't stop until they were in his bedroom.

"The bedroom? Seriously?" she asked, pulling her hand from his.

"It's just the quietest place at the moment," he said with ease. "Do you want to sit down?"

She shook her head, thankful for the glass of wine in her one hand while the other was still clutching the pashmina. "What's going on, Beckett? I don't understand any of this."

"When Ted went on his little tirade on Christmas Day, he made me take a hard look at my life. I knew I was a hard-ass; I actually enjoyed being one, but to listen to the way he talked about me, it bothered me. A lot. It was like every bad thing I ever thought about myself was confirmed. When you ran out of the room, he laid it on the line and told me that if I wasn't ready to give you everything you deserved, then I should let you go."

He took a nervous step toward her. "So I said all those horrible things to push you away. I needed you to make the decision to leave, to hate me, so that maybe it would make it easier on you."

"It was horrible, Beckett," she cried. "You have no idea how much it hurt to hear you say those things."

"I know, sweetheart, I know. And I'm so sorry. I wish I'd been stronger. I wish I was more confident about myself and being capable of being the man you deserve."

"So what's changed?" she asked quietly, staring at the wine in her glass.

"I missed you. I don't think I've ever missed someone the way I missed you. From the minute you walked out the door, I felt like I was dying. I should have stood up for myself, for you, for us. I don't know how I can ever make it up to you, but I want the chance to try. Please, Hope. Tell me I'm not too late. Tell me I didn't ruin this."

"What about all the things Ted said? What about your work schedule? The people in your life?"

"I called Logan and Julie on Christmas Day. It was one of the hardest things I've ever had to do. I've never asked anyone for their forgiveness, but I did to both of them. We all cried and then laughed and today is the first time I've seen both of them in years. I missed so much of their lives because of my own stubbornness. I don't want to keep missing out on life."

She gave a small shrug. "Okay, so…you made some calls to your family. That's an easy one."

"I gave Jerome his job back," he said, taking another step toward her.

"I know. We stopped by the office on our way here. Ted wanted to surprise me. Jerome told me how you called him personally and how you're going to help them find a specialist for his wife."

"Arlene," he said. "I'm hopeful with the right doctor she's going to start feeling a lot better."

Hope nodded. "I hope so. Jerome's a sweet

man. I'm sure his wife is a good person too."

"I have to admit, though, I didn't give your brother his job back."

Her head snapped up. "What?"

He shook his head. "Ted's over-qualified for the job he had. He's now the vice-president of our finance department. Fewer hours, paid vacations and holidays. He should have plenty of time to spend with his family and he's even going to have his wedding at our hotel on the Outer Banks. It was Merry's request."

Hope chuckled. "Just as long as she doesn't cater it, I'm sure it will be lovely." She took a sip of her wine. "Let me guess, Ted didn't tell me because you wanted to surprise me with it."

He nodded and finally closed the gap between them. "That's the last secret, Hope. Everything else is out there for the world to see."

"What about you? And your hours? Are you planning on cutting back?"

"Absolutely. I've promoted most of my executive staff. They'll all be taking on the responsibilities that should have been theirs before, but I kept holding on and trying to control everything. They're all qualified to run the company in my absence."

"Absence? Why? Where are you going?"

"I plan on taking a very lengthy vacation. The plan is to spend a month traveling and visiting as many of our resorts and hotels as possible just to check in."

She nodded. "That sounds like a good plan. There could be a lot of work involved in that. Just because you're not doing it from your office, it still counts as work."

Slowly, Beckett took the wine glass from her hand and placed it on the bedside table. Then he carefully unwrapped the pashmina from around her shoulders. And finally, he wrapped his arms around her waist and pulled her in close. "There won't be any time for work. I'll be too busy pampering the woman I love the way she deserves to be."

Her eyes went wide as she looked up at him, her mouth forming a perfect "o."

"I don't suppose it's possible that your boss would be willing to give you a month off for such a trip, is there?"

She smiled. "I have an in with the boss. I don't think it will be a problem."

Beckett visibly sagged with relief. "So that's a yes, right?"

Hope nodded.

"I love you, Hope Cooper. I love you more than I ever thought a man could love a woman. Thank you for coming into my life and saving me and giving me my life and my family back."

Reaching up, Hope cupped his cheek. "And I love you, G.B. James," she teased. "Thank you for showing me there is some goodness in the world and for giving me my hope for the future."

"That's what you are to me, my Hope."

Epilogue

Three months later…

"I thought you were done working."

"I am. Almost. Just a few more minutes, I swear."

Sigh. "We had a deal. No work after six. It's almost seven. Besides, dinner's just about ready."

"Okay, okay…I just need to do this one last thing and then I'll be done."

"Hope," Beckett said with mock annoyance. "I'm beginning to feel like you're taking me for granted. How can I compete with your computer? I mean, I slaved away in the kitchen and you can't even look away from your work."

"Aww…you're feeling neglected?" she teased as she shut down the computer and stood up and stretched. Walking over to him, she reached up and thoroughly kissed him on the lips. "I have this very demanding client who gave me a specification list a

231

mile long." She sighed. "Honestly, he's a complete beast to work for."

"Hey!" he said, putting his hands on his hips. "That list is not a mile long!" And he couldn't keep from laughing. "Okay, maybe it's a little long but I just know what the resort website needs. I want to make sure we don't miss anything. I want you to pay special attention to the café."

"I'm not going to miss a thing," she promised. "I do this every day and you need to trust me. And in case you've forgotten, I have a vested interest in that café. My name's on it."

"Of course I trust you," he said and wrapped his arms around her as he lowered his head to kiss her. "I just need to make sure it's right."

"Oh, you!" she said and pulled out of his arms. "Just for that, I'm going to use all bright, cartoony colors and forget to put the directions, address and name of the resort on there!"

Beckett swatted at her bottom and she screeched and ran from the room. He caught up with her instantly and scooped her up into his arms. He carried her to their bedroom and promptly dropped her on the bed.

"Okay, if I promise to stop bugging you and hovering over the work you're doing on the website, then there's something you'll need to do for me," he said seriously.

She looked up at him in confusion.

"Hope Cooper, I want you to marry me." He dropped to one knee beside the bed and pulled a black velvet box from his pocket. "I wanted to wait to ask you when we were up in the mountains next weekend, but I couldn't wait. I feel like I've been waiting for you my whole life and I don't want to wait anymore. Will you? Will you marry me? Be my wife?"

She couldn't speak. Instead, she sat up and launched herself into his arms as they tumbled to the floor. Beckett rolled her beneath him and kissed her thoroughly until they were both gasping for breath.

"I love you, Hope."

"I love you so much, Beckett. And there's nothing I want more in this world than to be your wife."

"I know it would kind of be stealing Ted and Merry's thunder, but I don't want to wait. Tell me how long it would take you to plan a wedding and let's do it. Whatever you want, I'll make it happen. I promise."

She chuckled. "Does it snow in the mountains in March?"

Beckett looked at her quizzically. "Sometimes. I guess. Why?"

"Because if I were to plan our perfect wedding, all I'd want is to be back up at your house in the mountains, with a million stars in the sky to match the millions of twinkly lights you have in the trees and to be married in the gazebo."

A wide grin crossed his face before he leaned in and kissed her again. "Your wish is my command. You name the date and it's yours."

"Next weekend."

"I don't think there's snow in the forecast."

"We'll pretend," she said, looking up into his dark eyes in amazement at the changes she'd seen in him since that fateful week they spent together.

"Or I can rent a snow machine and make sure that the ground is covered."

"Baby, as long as you're waiting for me in the gazebo, it doesn't matter if there's snow or not."

"I want to make all of your dreams come true."

"You already have, Beckett. The biggest dream come true of them all."

ABOUT THE AUTHOR

Samantha Chase is a New York Times and USA Today bestseller of contemporary romance. She released her debut novel in 2011 and currently has more than forty titles under her belt! When she's not working on a new story, she spends her time reading romances, playing way too many games of Scrabble or Solitaire on Facebook, wearing a tiara while playing with her sassy pug Maylene…oh, and spending time with her husband of 25 years and their two sons in North Carolina.

Where to Find Me:
Website: www.chasing-romance.com
Facebook:
www.facebook.com/SamanthaChaseFanClub
Twitter: https://twitter.com/SamanthaChase3
Amazon: http://amzn.to/2lhrtQa
Sign up for my mailing list and get exclusive content and chances to win members-only prizes!
http://bit.ly/1jqdxPR

Also by Samantha Chase

The Enchanted Bridal Series:

The Wedding Season
Friday Night Brides
The Bridal Squad

The Montgomery Brothers Series:

Wait for Me
Trust in Me
Stay with Me
More of Me
Return to You
Meant for You
I'll Be There

The Shaughnessy Brothers Series:

Made for Us
Love Walks In
Always My Girl
This is Our Song
Sky Full of Stars
Holiday Spice

Band on the Run Series:

One More Kiss

The Christmas Cottage Series:

The Christmas Cottage
Ever After

Silver Bell Falls Series:

Christmas in Silver Bell Falls
Christmas On Pointe

Life, Love & Babies Series:

The Baby Arrangement
Baby, Be Mine
Baby, I'm Yours

Preston's Mill Series:

Roommating
Speed Dating

The Protectors Series:

Duty Bound
Honor Bound
Forever Bound
Home Bound

Standalone Novels:

Jordan's Return
Catering to the CEO
In the Eye of the Storm
A Touch of Heaven
Moonlight in Winter Park

Wildest Dreams
Going My Way
Going to Be Yours
Waiting for Midnight
Seeking Forever
Mistletoe Between Friends
Snowflake Inn Wedding

NEW YORK TIMES & USA TODAY BESTSELLING AUTHOR

SAMANTHA
CHASE

Christmas in
Silver Bell Falls

A SILVER BELL FALLS HOLIDAY NOVELLA

Enjoy the following excerpt for

Christmas in Silver Bell
Falls

A Silver Bell Falls Holiday Novella

Chapter One

There was nothing quite like coming home at the end of a long day: kicking off your shoes…having a little something to eat while watching TV…and most importantly, not having to hear any more Christmas music!

Melanie Harper was certain she wasn't the only one who felt that way. It was early November and the holiday season was just getting under way.

"More like under my skin," she murmured as she walked into her kitchen and poured herself a glass of wine. Taking her glass, she went back to her living room and sat down on the couch.

It had been a long day. A long week. Hell, if she were being honest, it had been a long three months. With deadlines approaching, her editor was getting more and more snarky while Melanie was getting more and more discouraged.

Writer's block.

In her ten years of writing, she'd never once suffered from it, but for some reason the words refused to come.

"Figures," she said with disgust and turned on the TV. Flipping through the channels, it was all the same thing—Christmas specials, Christmas movies and holiday-themed shows. Unable to stand it, she turned it off and sighed.

It was always like this. Christmas. The holidays. Every year, if something bad was going to happen, it happened around Christmas.

Not that it had been that way her entire life, but…she stopped and paused. No, scratch that. It had been like that her entire life. Her earliest memory was of the Christmas when she was five. That was the year her mother left. Her father had been too distraught to celebrate that year so she spent the day watching him drink and cry.

There had been a glimmer of hope for the next year—her dad promised her it would be better. The flu had both of them fighting for the bathroom the entire day. And after that, it was all one big, giant blur of suckiness. Between financial struggles and family issues—and that one year where they had gotten robbed the day before Christmas—Melanie had come to see the months of November and December as nothing but a big nuisance. Eventually they stopped even attempting to celebrate.

And now she'd be able to add "getting cut by her publisher because of writer's block" to the Christmas resume of doom.

The name almost made her chuckle.

It would have been easy to sit there and wax unpoetic about how much she hated this time of the year, but a knock at the door saved her. Placing her wine glass down, she padded to the front door and pulled it open.

"Hey! There's my girl!"

Melanie smiled as her dad wrapped her in his embrace. "Hey, Dad." She hugged him back and then stepped aside so he could come in. "What's going on? I thought we were getting together on

Saturday for dinner."

John Harper smiled at his only child as he took off his coat. "Is this a bad time?"

She shook her head. "No, not at all. I just wasn't expecting you. Have you eaten dinner yet?"

He chuckled softly. "It's almost eight, Mel. Of course I have." He studied her for a minute. "Don't tell me you haven't."

She shrugged. "It was a long day and I sort of lost my appetite."

"Uh-oh. What happened?"

Melanie led him to the living room and sat down on the couch again. "My deadline will be here at the end of December and I haven't written a thing."

"Okay," he said slowly. "So…can't they extend your deadline?"

She shook her head. "They've extended it three times already."

"Hmm…so what's the problem with the story? Why are you having such a hard time with it? That's not like you."

She sighed again. "They're pretty much demanding a Christmas story."

"Oh."

She didn't even need to look at him to know his expression was just as pinched as hers at the topic. "Yeah…oh."

"Did you try explaining…?"

Nodding, she sat up and reached for her glass of wine. "Every time I talk to them. They don't get it and they don't care. Basically their attitude is that I'm a fiction writer and I should be able to use my

242

imagination to concoct this Christmas story without having to draw on personal experience."

"Maybe they don't realize just how much you dislike the holiday."

"Dislike is too mild of a word," she said flatly. Taking a long drink, she put her glass down and looked at him. "I don't even want to talk about it. The meeting with my editor and agent went on and on and on today so my brain is pretty fried. The only thing to come out of it is yet another crappy reinforcement of the holiday."

"Oh, dear…"

Melanie's eyes narrowed. "What? What's wrong?"

"I guess maybe I should have called first because…" He stopped. "You know what? Never mind. We'll talk on Saturday." He stood quickly and walked back toward the foyer.

"Oh, no," she said as she went after him. "You can't come here and say something like that and then leave! Come on. What's going on?"

John sighed and reached for her hand. "Your grandmother died."

Melanie simply stared at him for a minute. "Oh…okay. Wow. Um…when?"

"A month ago."

Her eyes went wide. "And you're just telling me now?"

Slowly, he led her back to the couch. "Mel, seriously? Your grandmother hasn't spoken to me in over twenty-five years. I'm surprised I was notified."

"I guess," she sighed. Then she looked at him.

"Are you okay?"

He shrugged. "I'm not sure. I always thought when the time came that it wouldn't mean anything. After all, she kind of died to me all those years ago. But now? Now that I know she's really gone?" His voice choked with emotion. "It all suddenly seems so stupid, so wrong. I mean, how could I have let all those years go by without trying to make things right?"

Squeezing his hand, Melanie reached over and hugged him. "It's not like you never tried, Dad. Grandma was pretty stubborn. You can't sit here and take all the blame."

When she released him, she saw him wipe away a stray tear. "In my mind, I guess I always thought there would be time. Time to make amends and…"

"I know," she said softly. "And I'm sorry. I really am."

"You probably don't even remember her. You were so little when it all happened."

It was the truth, sort of. Melanie had some memories of her grandmother and none of them were of the warm and fuzzy variety. Unfortunately, now wasn't the time to mention it. "So who contacted you?"

"Her attorney. He actually called last night and met me in person today."

"Well that was nice of him. I guess."

"He had some papers for me. For us."

Melanie looked at him oddly. "What kind of papers?"

"She um…she left some things to us in her

will."

Her eyes went wide again. "Seriously? The woman didn't talk to either of us all these years and she actually put us in her will? Is it bad stuff?"

John chuckled. "What do you mean by bad stuff?"

"You know…like she has a really old house and she was a hoarder and we're supposed to clean it out. Or she has some sort of vicious pet we're supposed to take care of. That kind of thing."

John laughed even harder. "Sometimes your imagination really is wild; you know that, right?" he teased.

Melanie couldn't help but laugh with him. "What? It's true! Things like that happen all the time!"

"Mel, it doesn't," he said, wiping the tears of mirth from his eyes. "And for your information, there was no hoarding, no vicious pets…"

"Did she collect dead animals or something?"

He laughed again. "No. Nothing like that."

Relaxing back on the couch, she looked at her father. "Okay. Lay it on me then. What could she possibly have put in her will for the two of us?"

John took a steadying breath. "She left me my father's coin collection."

That actually made Melanie smile. "I know how much you used to talk about it." She nodded with approval. "That's a good gift to get."

He nodded. "She'd kept it all these years. Then there's some family photos, things from my childhood that she had saved, that sort of thing."

"So no money," Melanie said because she

already knew the answer.

John shook his head. "And it's fine with me. I don't think I would have felt comfortable with it. All those years ago, it would have meant the world to me to have a little help so you and I didn't have to struggle so much. But we're good now and I don't really need or want it."

"Who'd she leave it to? Her cat? Some snooty museum?"

"Museums aren't snooty," he said lightly.

"Anyway," she prompted. "So who'd she leave her fortune to?"

With a sigh he took one of her hands in his. "She left the bulk of her estate to the local hospice care center."

"Oh…well…that was nice of her," Melanie said. "I guess she wasn't entirely hateful."

"No, she wasn't," John said softly. "And she did leave you something."

The statement wasn't a surprise since he'd mentioned it earlier, but Melanie figured he'd tell her when he was ready.

"When the attorney told me about it," he began, "I was a little surprised. I had no idea she still had it."

Curiosity piqued, she asked, "Had what?"

"The cabin."

Okay, *that* was a surprise, she thought. "Grandma had a cabin? Where?"

"Up north. Practically on the border of Canada."

"Seriously? Why on earth would she have a cabin there?"

A small smile played across John's face. "Believe it or not, there was a time when your grandmother wasn't quite so…hard. She loved the winters and loved all of the outdoor activities you could do in the snow. She skied, went sleigh riding and…get this…she loved Christmas."

Pulling her hand from his, Melanie stood with a snort of disgust. "That's ironic. The woman went out of her way to ruin so many of our Christmases and now you're telling me she used to love them? So…so…what? She started hating them after I came along? That would just be the icing on the rotten Christmas cookie."

John came to his feet and walked over to her. Placing his hands on her shoulders, he turned her to look at him. "It wasn't you, sweetheart. It was me. When your mom left, grandma wanted us to move in with her—but there were conditions and rules and I just knew it wasn't the kind of environment I wanted you to grow up in."

"Dad, I know all this. I remember the fights but…what made her hate Christmas?"

He shook his head. "She didn't. As far as I know, she always loved it."

"Then…then why? Why would she ruin ours?"

A sad expression covered his face. "It was punishment. I grew up loving Christmas and we always made such a big celebration out of it. It was her way of punishing me for not falling in line. She took away that joy."

Tears filled Melanie's eyes. "See? She was hateful. And whatever this cabin thing is, I don't want it."

"Mel…"

"No, I'm serious!" she interrupted. "I don't want anything from her. She ruined so many things in our lives because she was being spiteful! Why on earth would I accept anything from her?"

"Because I think you need it," he said, his tone firm, serious.

"Excuse me?"

Leading her back to the sofa, they sat down. "I think this may have come at the perfect time."

She rolled her eyes. "Seriously?"

"Okay, that didn't quite come out the way I had planned," he said with a chuckle. "What I meant is…I think you could really use the time away. With the pressure you're feeling about the book, maybe a change of scenery will really help put things into perspective."

"Dad," Melanie began, "a change of scenery is not going to undo twenty-five years of hating Christmas. And besides, I really don't want the…the cabin. I don't want anything from her. It would have meant more to me to have her in my life while she was alive."

He sighed. "I know and I wish things could have been different. But…this is really something you need to do."

She looked at him with disbelief. "Now I *need* to do it? Why?"

"Melanie, you are my daughter and I love you."

"That's an ominous start."

"You're too young to be this disillusioned and angry. We can't go back and change anything, but I think you need to do this to make peace with the past and have some hope for the future."

"Dad..."

"Three months, Mel, that's all I'm asking."

She jumped to her feet. "You expect me to go live in some arctic place for three months? Are you crazy?"

He smiled patiently at her. "I'm not crazy and you know I'm right."

"No...I'm still going with crazy."

"There's a stipulation in the will," he began cautiously.

"What kind of stipulation?"

"You need to live in the cabin for three months. After that, you're free to sell it."

"That's a bunch of bull. What if I don't want to live there at all? Why can't I just sell it now? Or give it away?"

"If you don't want it, it will be given away."

"Well then...good riddance."

"You're being spiteful just for the sake of it, Mel. What have you got to lose? You work from home so you don't have that hanging over your head and your condo is paid for. Think of it as a writing retreat. Your editor will love the idea and it will show how you're seriously trying to get the book done. It's a win-win if you think about it."

"Ugh," she sighed. "I'm not a big fan of being cold."

"The cabin has heat."

"It will mean I'll be gone for Christmas."

He chuckled. "Nice try. We don't celebrate it anymore, remember?"

She let out a small growl of frustration. "I'm

still going to have writer's block. That's not going to change."

"Trust me. It will."

Tilting her head, she gave him a curious look. "What's that supposed to mean?"

"Okay, there really isn't any way *not* to tell you this…"

"Tell me what?"

"The town is pretty much all about Christmas."

"Forget it. I'm not going." She sat back down and crossed her arms.

"You're too old to pout so knock it off," he said.

She glared at her father. "So I'm supposed to go to this…this…Christmas town and then, thanks to the wonder of it all, suddenly I'm going to be able to write this fabulous holiday story and have it become a bestseller?"

"There's that imagination again! I knew it was still in there!"

"Ha-ha. Very funny." Slouching down she let out another growl. "I really don't want to do this."

"Mel, it's not often that I put my foot down. You're normally more level-headed and you're old enough that I don't need to, but this time, I'm going to have to put my foot down."

"Who gets the cabin if I turn it down?"

John sighed dejectedly. "I have no idea. The lawyer didn't say."

"Maybe she left it to someone who really needs it," Melanie said, trying to sound hopeful.

"She did," John replied. "You."

∝⤝⤞

A week later, Melanie was in her car and driving halfway across the country to see if she could get her writing mojo back. It was a fifteen-hour drive so she split it up over two days and since she was alone in the car, she had nothing to do but think.

"She couldn't have left me a condo in Hawaii or maybe someplace tropical like the Bahamas? No. I have to go to the tip of freaking New York for this." It was a running dialogue in her head throughout the drive and it seemed like the closer she got, the angrier she became.

On the second day of the trip, when her GPS told her she was less than an hour away from her destination, she called her father and put him on speakerphone.

"Hey, sweetheart! How's the drive?"

"She hated me," Melanie replied. "She seriously hated me."

"I'm not even going to pretend I don't know who you're referring to," he said. "Are you there already? Is the cabin in bad shape?"

"I'm not there yet but I'm driving on this little two-lane road and there is nothing out here. I mean nothing! The GPS says I should be there soon but I haven't seen a city or a town in quite a while. Where am I supposed to shop and get food? Or am I supposed to hunt for it? Because if I am, that's a deal-breaker and you should have told me."

John laughed. "You seriously need to put all of this in your book. It's hysterical!"

"I'm not trying to be funny here, Dad! I'm serious! There isn't anything around!"

"You haven't gotten there yet. If I remember correctly, there are plenty of places to shop and eat. You won't starve and you certainly won't have to go out and kill your dinner so don't worry."

"But you don't know that for sure…"

"Mel, stop looking for trouble. We talked about this. It's going to be good for you. Your editor is thrilled and promised to give you a little extra time so you're off to a promising start."

"Yeah…I'm lucky," Melanie deadpanned.

"You need a positive attitude, young lady," he admonished. "I'm serious. I want you to make the most of this time you have up there."

She mentally sighed. "I'll try, Dad. But I'm not making any promises."

"That's all I ask."

"Okay, well…let me go because the road seems to be getting pretty winding and hilly and I need to pay attention to it. I'll call you when I get there."

"Be safe, sweetheart!"

Hanging up, Melanie frowned at the road. It was getting narrower and the sky was getting a little bit darker. A chill went down her spine and attributing it to the cooling temperatures, she cranked up the heat.

The GPS began calling out directions to her and Melanie feared she was leaving civilization further and further behind. "I better hit the *New York Times* for this," she murmured. A few minutes later she hit the brakes and stared at the giant sign on the side of the road.

"Silver Bell Falls Welcomes You!"

Melanie frowned and then looked around because she was certain she was hearing things. Turning down her car stereo, she groaned when she heard the song "Silver Bells" coming from the massive sign.

City sidewalks, busy sidewalks, dressed in holiday style…in the air there's a feeling of Christmas…

"You have got to be kidding me." Cranking the radio up to block out the Christmas carol, Melanie slammed her foot on the gas and continued her drive. It was maybe only a mile down the road when she spotted a small grocery store, a gas station and a diner.

And that was it.

"I guess I just drove through town," she sighed. It was tempting to stop and look around but she was anxious to get to the house and check it out first. Being practical, Melanie had already shopped for enough food and essentials to get her by for the first night. And besides, she had no idea what kind of shape the house was going to be in.

"Turn left," the GPS directed and Melanie did just that. "Your destination is at the end of the road."

Squinting, Melanie looked straight ahead but saw…nothing. There were trees, lots and lots of trees. Slowing down, she approached the end of the pavement and saw a dirt road that led through the trees and a small mailbox hidden in the brush.

"Charming." With no other choice, she carefully drove off the pavement and made her way over the bumpy road through the trees. It was like a dense forest and for a minute, she didn't think she was going to get through it.

But then she did.

The field opened up and off to the right was a house—not a cabin. In her mind, Melanie pictured some sort of log cabin, but the structure she was looking at was more stone than log. It was a one-story home with a wraparound porch and a red roof. The yard was completely manicured and the place even looked like it had a fresh coat of paint.

Since neither she nor her father had any contact with her grandmother, there was no way for them to know about the upkeep on the place. She had tried to question the lawyer, but other than giving her the deed to the house and the keys, he had very little information for her.

A little beyond the house was a shed. It looked like it was perched on a trailer and it certainly looked a lot newer than the house. Maybe it had been a new addition. Maybe her grandmother hadn't known she was going to die and was doing some renovations on the property.

Pulling up to the front of the house, Melanie sighed. She was anxious to go and explore the space and silently prayed she wasn't going to open the door to some sort of nightmare. Climbing from the car, the first thing she did was stretch. Looking around the property from where she stood, the only thing that was obvious to her was that she had no neighbors—she couldn't even see another house!

Pulling the key from her pocket, she closed the car door and carefully walked up the two steps to the front porch. Stopping at the front door, she bounced on her feet and noticed that the floor was in pretty good shape—no creaking and a lot of the wood looked fairly new.

Not a bad start, she thought and opened the front door.

Stopping dead in her tracks, she could only stare. It was dark and dusty and there was a smell that made her want to gag. Not that she was surprised, but it did cause her to spring into action. With a hand over her mouth, she quickly made her way around the house opening windows. Next, she went out to her car and grabbed the box of cleaning supplies out of the trunk. Melanie knew a certain amount of cleaning would be involved, but she hadn't expected quite so much.

For the next three hours she scrubbed and dusted and vacuumed and mopped. It didn't matter that it was thirty degrees outside, and currently pushing that temperature inside thanks to the open windows; she was sweating. Once she was satisfied with the way things looked, she walked outside, grabbed the box of linens and went about making the bed. Next came the groceries and finally her own personal belongings.

It was dark outside and every inch of Melanie's body hurt. Slowly she made her way back around the house to close the windows and jacked up the heat. Luckily the fireplace was gas, clearly a recent update. She flipped the switch and sighed with relief when it roared to life and the blower immediately began pushing out heat as well.

Guzzling down a bottle of water, she looked

around with a sense of satisfaction. The house was small, maybe only a thousand square feet, but it had potential. Grabbing a banana from her cooler, she peeled and ate it while contemplating her next move.

"Shower," she finally said. "A nice hot shower or maybe a bath." The latter sounded far more appealing. Locking the front door, Melanie walked to the newly-cleaned bathroom and started the bath water. It was a fairly decent-sized tub and for that she was grateful. "Bath salts," she murmured and padded to the master bedroom to search through her toiletry bag.

Within minutes, the bathroom was steamy and fragrant and Melanie could feel the tension starting to leave her body. Her cell phone rang and she cursed when she realized she had forgotten to call her father when she'd arrived.

"Hey, Dad!" she said quickly. "Sorry!"

He chuckled. "Are you all right?"

"I am. The house was a mess and once I got inside and looked around, I couldn't help but start cleaning. I guess I lost track of the time."

"Have you eaten dinner yet?" he asked expectantly.

"A banana."

"Mel…" he whined. "You have to start taking better care of yourself."

"I will. I know. Actually, I'm just getting ready to take a nice hot bath to relax. I promise I'll eat as soon as I'm done."

He sighed wearily. "Okay. Be sure that you do. Call me tomorrow."

"I will, Dad. Thanks."

She hung up and turned the water off. Looking around, Melanie grabbed some fresh towels from one of her boxes and set them on the vanity before stripping down and gingerly climbing into the steamy water. A groan of pure appreciation escaped her lips as soon as she was fully submerged.

"This almost makes up for all the grime," she sighed and rested her head back, closing her eyes. "Heavenly."

For a few minutes, Melanie let her mind be blank and simply relaxed. The hot water and the salts were doing wonders for her tired body and it was glorious. Then, unable to help herself, her mind went back into work mode. A running list of supplies she was going to need was first and she cursed not having a pad and pen handy to start writing things down. Next came the necessities of going into town and maybe meeting her neighbors.

And then there was the book.

The groan that came out this time had nothing to do with relaxation and everything to do with dread. "Damn Christmas story. Why can't I write what I want to write?" It was something she'd been asking her editor for months and the only response she got was how all of the other in-house authors were contributing to building their holiday line, and she would be no exception. "Stupid rule."

And then something came to her.

Melanie sat up straight in the tub and only mildly minded the water that sloshed over the side of the tub. "All I need to do is write a story that takes place around Christmas. It doesn't have to necessarily be about Christmas!" Her heart began to beat frantically. "I've been focusing on the wrong thing!" Relief swamped her and she forced herself to relax again. Sinking back into the water, she closed her eyes and let her mind wander to all of the possibilities that had suddenly opened up.

"A romance at Christmas time," she said quietly. "Major emphasis on romance, minor on Christmas. Technically, I'm meeting my obligations." She smiled. "Hmm…a heroine alone—maybe stranded—in a winter storm and a sexy hero who storms in and rescues her."

Melanie purred. "Yeah. That could definitely work." Sinking further down into the water, an image of the hero came to mind. Tall. That was a given. Muscular, but not overly so. Maybe lean would be a better way to describe him. And dark hair. She was a sucker for the dark hair. "Sex on a stick," she said quietly, enjoying the image that was playing in her mind.

The bathroom door swung open and Melanie's eyes flew open as she screamed. The man standing in the doorway seemed to have stepped almost completely from her imagination. If she wasn't so freaking scared at the moment, she would appreciate it.

"I wouldn't count on sex on a stick or anyplace else if I were you. You're trespassing and you're under arrest."

CPSIA information can be obtained
at www.ICGtesting.com
Printed in the USA
BVHW04s2231180318
510940BV00008B/124/P